Maqoom

Richard Morrison

Look Up Publishing—Bainbridge, GA
ISBN: 978-1-7364273-0-9
Library of Congress Control Number: 2020925987
Title: Maqoom
Author: Richard Morrison
Digital distribution | 2021
Paperback | 2021

Dedication

To the Judge of all the earth, thank You for Israel who has been doing their duty, in teaching us of You. I am a witness, that indeed, Israel is here doing what he is to do. Also, thank You for the woman You blessed me with for a wife, as Shalom stood opposite me for almost a full year caringly, patiently standing steadfast on that which was the proper road; immovable until I would either turn and come along or alone, she would go without me. What love You have expressed towards me through both Israel and the woman You blessed me with as a wife.

Introduction

First off, I am a Noahide. A gentile, who has acknowledged and accepted the seven Noahide laws that G-d gave to Noah, hence to all humanity.

The foundation of the book is the word in Hebrew that means "The Place," the place where Infinity meets the finite, where G-d meets finite man. Transliterated I did into English as Maqoom, מקום. It is my belief that any human can get to that place, whether Jewish or Gentile. The sincerity, the desire to be one with G-d, to be like G-d in one's character, manners and treatment of fellow humans.

Maqoom can be useful to both Jewish and Gentile peoples. It crosses the divide to the reality that Israel is G-d's chosen, but all peoples can come to G-d and Israel is there to teach us and bring us closer.

The main theme of this particular manuscript is gratitude. Gratitude to G-d for all things.

There are definitely some who would not like the killing that occurs in this book. However, I deem it as a reality of the Realm of Existence we currently reside in on this Earth at this time, believing it is a tool with which to show others, that true Shalom can only come by eliminating that which is keeping you from Shalom, as long as one does so within the confines of G-d's creation and laws and Will.

Chapter 1
Father's Home

K thunk, as the wedge of the axe forced itself into the fibers of the wood. Maqoom liked chopping wood. It would stretch his shoulders and back. Would allow him to concentrate on a specific spot on the top of the wood, with which to place the wedge of the axe, helping his coordination and concentration. In addition, it helped to tone his arm muscles, aiding in the holding steady of the rifle and pistol, when his dad would take him shooting. He wanted to please his dad in this, as it seemed to be the only activity that they got to spend together, in which his dad showed interest. He had been chopping for at least two hours so far today.

The day was astounding, to be out and a part of it. When he first stepped out of the house to tend to the animals, the air was still cool from the evening chill. Inside the house was warm, as the breakfast fire had been burning, but outside the night air was still clinging to the earth, and it felt good going across the skin of his cheeks and going up into his nostrils with each inhalation. He smiled and looked at the beautiful blue sky. Just one or two small clouds here and there, but almost all blue and open. So open, like it could go on forever. But of course, he knew that was not true. As his mother had taught him, that creation had its limits, as it is all contained within the Creator. His smile got bigger, as he thought of the awesomeness of the Creator, Who could create all this, and Who was the true Infinity. He paused for a moment thinking of this and feeling the coolness of the air and seeing the sight of the expansive blue sky. He turned his head ever so slightly, to allow the breeze to whish past his ear in such a way, as to allow him to hear the breeze. The sound was so strong, like a mini tornado inside his ear canal. It reminded him of the time he sat on the edge of some flooded timber, as the sun was going down in the West, when a small flock of ducks, came in, to roost. The ducks had their wings locked out, gliding through the air, coming in for a landing on the water. As some went directly over his head, within two to three feet, as well as one or two off to each side of his head, the sound of their wings breaking the cohesion of the air, stirring up turbulence as the air went over and under their wing feathers, sounded very similar to this current sound in his ear canal, but much stronger. He tried to mimic the sound later as he told his mother, but he gave it no justice. Even a train going very close by at full speed, did not compare. But, turning his head, ever so slightly into the wind, would be close enough to make him smile at the remembrance. He was just a very small part of the whole, with gratefulness within him for the opportunity and ability to acknowledge such.

"Maqoom, wash up for breakfast!"

"Ok Mom!"

He did not realize he was hungry, but now that the thought had been given to him, he realized how hungry he was.

As Maqoom's mother, Sarah, closed the door and turned towards the dining table, her husband Frank was looking up from his gun cleaning chore, straight in her eyes.

"I told you not to call him that! His name is Malcom."

"Well, you have been away for almost four months, and I like it so much for what it means, that I digressed and started calling him that about two months ago or so. I am sorry."

Frank went back to his cleaning and Sarah walked over to the kettle of stew hanging over the fire. Fresh vegetables and venison, one of Maqoom's favorites.

Frank's cohort Hans was sitting on the sofa, over by the wall with Frank at the table between them. Sarah liked having as much room as possible between her and Hans. A devil of a man. Thin, scraggly, whose teeth were almost non-existent except for a discolored one here or there. Breath as foul as what she presumed the Devil's would be. One time, while all were at the table, he laughed so hard at one of Frank's jokes that his breath reached Sarah, who almost gagged, but managed to keep it under control. He laughs like what she thinks a gargoyle would laugh like; high pitched and broken, with eyes flirting about, like he knows something that you don't, which seems to excite him, making the laugh even higher pitched. He is always glancing looks at her from the sides of his eyes or while looking up when facing down, never straight on.

Frank and Han's have been riding together for about the last five years now. Both take such care of their guns, like they love them more than any human. They both handle them very well too. Which worries Sarah somewhat, as with Frank's guidance, Maqoom is showing great promise with the weapons, and his father Frank is taking notice. She knows Maqoom wants to please him, which is normal for a son towards his father; but she had hoped for another way that Maqoom could please his father, other than proficiency with a gun.

Sarah wants out so bad, but it is not her makeup to quit, nor can she give a second thought to leaving Maqoom, to be totally raised by his Father. Just as she is throwing the thought out of her consciousness, Maqoom walks in the door.

"Oh, that smells delicious Mom!"

He has such a big smile on this face that it makes her smile too.

"It is so beautiful outside Mom, just glorious. Makes one just know that the Creator is present."

Frank bristles and sternly asks, "Son what did I tell you about talking religion around me?"

Malcom and Sarah both lose their smiles. Malcom reflects a moment then apologizes to his father, telling him, "I am sorry Dad."

Frank goes on a small tirade. "Just because I am out of the house and away from the property for a period of months, you two cannot decide on your own to break the rules. So, I don't really mean nuthin to either one of you, huh? Oh, if I meant somethin to ya, you would not hurt me so, with such rebellion. Even when I am away you would keep my rules. Have to sit and think a spell, how I am going to correct this!"

Maqoom is standing, reflecting on his dad's words wondering if he really is the bad one in all this, or is it his own Father?

Sarah states that she is going to put her sweater on, and then serve the food. Sarah heads towards the bedroom door, which is wide open and is directly off the kitchen. The kitchen, dining and living area all being one room, with the parent's bedroom being off the dining area and Maqoom's off the opposite corner.

Just as Sarah clears the doorway, Hans with a half-breath voice says, "Frank!" Frank looks at him, with

Hans motioning with his head towards the bedroom door, stating at the same time, "You owe me!"

Frank pauses, then says low, "Ok," looking back towards his gun cleaning.

Maqoom has worked his way to the sink behind Frank, getting a glass of drinking water. He hears what has been said, seeing out of the corner of his eye, without hesitation, Hans standing up, putting his gun in its holster, then starting to unbuckle his gun belt, while pivoting towards the bedroom door. Maqoom's heart is pounding so hard he can hear it beating in his ears. As his hands cling to the sink wall, his heart is beating so strong that it is making his body wave back and forth, ever so slightly but noticeable to him. His mind is almost blank. He looks straight out the window over the sink, then he realizes that he knows Hans has put the bullets back in the cylinder of the revolver before first speaking to Frank. He calms down, the beating heart smooths out, the waving stops and his grip on the sink loosens. He is fully aware how calm he is, not sure why, but like he is in the most serene, safest place in the world.

He smoothly and intently turns towards the bedroom door. Keenly aware of his dad's position, with full attention focused on Han's hanging gun belt. Hans walked silently through the bedroom doorway, as he did, he slipped his gun belt onto the wall mounted gun belt holder Maqoom's dad had put there the last time he was home. It was shoulder level for his dad, head high for Maqoom. Maqoom's movement was with full, focused intent, on what he was doing. As he closed in on the gun, he lifted his right hand, grabbing the outside gun by the handle, pulling it out smoothly, quietly but not slowly, with intent. He realized again how calm he was at this moment. Like this is what he was made for, or like he has done it a thousand times before.

Sarah gives out a scream, yelling "Frank help!" "Hans get away from me!"

Three more steps and Maqoom is well in the bedroom. Hans has a hand on each of Sarah's upper arms, squeezing to hang onto the squirming woman. Three more steps and Maqoom was half-way between the door and Hans. Maybe only ten feet away. Hans was so busy trying to kiss the woman, he knew of nothing else going on.

"Get your hands off my mother!" Maqoom said, just loud enough for Hans to hear.

Hans speed in turning made Maqoom take notice. He was fast, fully facing him in what seemed like a blur. The woman forgotten. Hans was in his element now, like Maqoom was, but Hans had the experience and confidence to allow him to be aware of it. Not so Maqoom, even though he was fully calm, he did not fully realize at this point, as to why or how, it just was.

Hans said, "Boy I am going to hurt you bad. That is my gun!"

With that Hans came at him, with a full frontal, head on attack. He must have thought the boy could not do it, or that he would miss because of the speed and the maneuvering Hans was doing with his head and upper torso. Maqoom was calm, his hand with the gun following Hans center point between his eyes. Maqoom squeezed the trigger with the gun bursting forth lead, fire and smoke. The crack of the blast going off inside the room, making Maqoom's ears ring immediately. The bullet caught Hans on the inside of his right eye, almost bursting it out of its socket, with the pressure and speed of the bullet pushing the lead projectile forward and further into his head. Because he was somewhat scrunched down as he was attacking, the bullet exited the back of the skull about the same level as it went in. Kathunk, the bullet hit the wood of the house, making Maqoom think of the axe hitting the wood. Hans hit the floor dead without even a jerk or any further motion.

"Malcom!" His dad yells behind him.

Maqoom spins immediately, not swinging the gun wide, but bending his elbow, bringing the gun by his side, so that if it was necessary to shoot right away, at least the barrel would be pointing in the correct direction, even if his arm was not extended. The flow of his hand and gun was smooth. He realized his Father was not attacking right away and that he had time to straighten his arm, bringing the gun out and up, to point the end of the barrel at his Father's face. Frank cocks his head slightly, looking at Maqoom's eyes.

"You going to shoot your own Father son? You really believe I did not know that you walked away from the sink to the bedroom? That you took Hans gun from its holster? This was a test and you passed. Now you and I can ride together son."

"I heard Hans tell you that you owed him, with you allowing him to come in here. No where can I see clearly, how you and I will ever be Father and son again!"

Frank made his move. Just as smooth and fast as Hans but even more determined, more experienced than Hans, like liquid Maqoom thought. Even in this blink of an eye action, Maqoom's brain was processing, consciously giving Maqoom a feeling of pride in his dad, as to how well he flowed in his movement. Like it wasn't just a bursting forth of a human body, but an intellectual maneuvering, that was inherently engrained within him through experience and confidence. When Hans made his move, it was as if everything slowed down for Maqoom.

He knew what was happening, with no blurs or movements missed by his consciousness. So too, now with his dad. Frank was closer to Maqoom when he started than what Hans had been. Two steps and already his hand was coming up to grab the gun, to push it away, while his other hand, in a fist was heading towards Maqoom's side. Maqoom followed that center of the eyes, with the gun firing only inches away from Frank's face. The bullet caught him on the bridge of the nose, with the pressure pushing both eyes out of their sockets ending in two bulging eyeballs, bloodshot to boot. Continuing in at an angle, going through the brain and out his right ear. The bullet's force pushing his head back while the body's momentum was propelling it forward. Frank hit the wall and floor about the same time, hard. The body actually bouncing off both almost simultaneously, ever so slightly sliding, then settling. Maqoom could see the right ear missing, basically ripped to shreds and splattered over the wall, as well as the brain material with some skin and bone. Frank was hard dead. No movement from him either, just like Hans.

Maqoom turned to look at his mother. She had both hands up, fingers touching, up over her mouth. Mouth half agape and eyes wide, holding her breath, it seemed to Maqoom. Sarah's eyes locked on Frank. Maqoom took note of his own physiology, noting that his heart was calm. He was not shaking, nor was he cold or hot. Mouth closed, breathing through his nostrils, in what seemed like normal breaths. Hands not shaking. He was calm!

"Mother," he called out softly. No response. "Eema," he said.

Sarah looked up, right at his eyes, her arms relaxing, with hands going to her sides, allowing the air captured in her lungs to escape. Maqoom could hear her breath leave, the breath of life he thought to himself, smiling with the musing. Maqoom, consciously aware of his smile, wondered how, after what just transpired, how he could allow himself to smile? Truth is the truth, no matter what else is occurring, truth stays the same. Maqoom took extreme comfort in that the Creator does not change, does not stray right or left, but is absolute. He kept his smile, trusting if he was wrong, that he would be taught appropriately. He was not sure how his mother would react. But by the time his thoughts were coming back to the now, his mother spoke up, calmly but with concern.

"Maqoom, are you alright?"

"Yes Mother, I'm alright, and you?" His smile broadening.

Sarah nodded her head yes, up and down, no audible sound. Then her thoughts came across her lips. "Why am I smiling?"

Maqoom heard, stating, "Because you are at peace Mother. It was not with intent, it was not planned, but it was the right thing to do."

She looked straight at him, straightening up her posture as if she was going to march.

Maqoom spoke next. "What I feared the most was what you would think of me. If you would hate me. It crossed my mind as I was squeezing the first shot, especially after shooting Dad."

"Maqoom, you saved me from a deranged maniac," looking at Hans, "A spiritually decrepitate, immoral beast of a man," then looking at Frank. "There is no ill will towards you at all my son. There is gratefulness to Heaven for you and what you were willing to do. Thank you Maqoom!"

"So be it!" Maqoom said. "I'll get the bodies out of here and get them buried."

It was three in the morning before Maqoom got the job done. He put them both in the same hole, side by side on their backs. The hole was about three feet deep. Enough to allow their bodies to go back to dust and keep the animals from getting them.

When he walked back into the house, Sarah was asleep at the table. She awoke with a start, as the door closed and was latched. "Why don't you go to bed Mother?"

"I will, now that you are back in the house. Are you finished with the chore?"

"Yes, the bodies are buried and I am ready to get some sleep."

"Good night Maqoom!"

"Good night Mother!"

Chapter 2
The Separation

When he awoke, it was already past midmorning. He felt lazy getting up so late, but he had an excuse he believed valid, not going to bed until after three. As he stepped out of his room, he could hear his mother in her room, in what sounded like she was trying to move furniture. He called out to her, "Mother." The noise stopped and she stepped out into the room.

"Have some breakfast for you Maqoom. Some fresh eggs, potatoes and beef."

"Thank you Mother!"

"What is the noise I hear you making from within your room?"

"Frank would come back sometimes and close the bedroom door, latching it from the inside. I could hear furniture move around, but of course I never dared ask him what he was doing. So, now I am moving furniture around to try to determine what he was doing. After you eat Maqoom, would you help me move the bed?"

"Of course Mother."

The meal was delicious, he was famished. Saying his blessing before the meal, giving thanks after made his mom smile broad. She was very proud of him and grateful for him. As he walked into the room, he noticed the bed was slightly askew, so he stated, "This must have been what you were trying to move when I heard you."

"Yes," Sarah stated. "There is no reason to move furniture unless you are putting something under the floor that the furniture is on. So that is what we are looking for. Some hint that the floorboards are not what they seem."

Maqoom had to move the heavy chest at the foot of the bed, then helping his mother push against the solid wood frame bed, they slid the bed off to the side of the room. They walked and stomped their feet on the floor, with it only taking minutes to find some boards that were not as secure as those around them. Maqoom got a claw hammer, prying the boards up to reveal a hole about three feet deep and four feet square. Just about as deep as he buried his dad, he thought. The hole was filled from side to side with burlap bags, so they pulled one up and untied the binding string. Cash! Lots of cash. Mostly twenties, but some other denominations in there too. By the time they got done counting, the figure Maqoom had in his head was over $14,000.

"$14,200," Sarah verbalized, before Maqoom could get out what he was thinking. "Maqoom, I have to believe it is all stolen. Never have I seen your Father actually work to sell any item or produce. Not even an animal. He would disappear for months at a time, always coming back, with the eventual result of him locking himself in the bedroom. Maqoom, what do you say we do with it?"

He did not take long to answer, couple seconds really, "We have to give it back!"

Sarah smiled. "Yes Maqoom, we have to give it back." She was so joyful over her son's answer. This was her son, not Frank's. "Maqoom, I have decided, must have actually decided months ago, but did not know how to make it happen, that I am going back East to my parents. The last letter I received was only about six weeks ago, and they are both thankfully, in fine health. It is my desire to go back and be with them."

This made Maqoom smile broadly, "Oh that would be swell Mother. It gives me such joy to hear this from you."

"Well, you are coming with me, aren't you Maqoom? We can take the money to the closest sheriff and be on our way. We will sell the farm and that should get us plenty for the journey. It is a nice chunk of land. Just right for farming, animals and a family."

"No Mother, it is my desire to take the money back. To each town. Find out what was taken and give it back."

Her enthusiasm faded somewhat, but she was still joyful over her son's desire to make a wrong into a right.

"Well son, will you stay until the land is sold, think it over and give me your final decision then?"

"Yes Mother, I'll think it over."

The closest town to them was about 50 miles south. When Sarah went there to advertise the farm, she enquired about any robberies and there were none in that town for over 15 years. Longer than what Maqoom has been on the earth. Nothing anyone really remembers or wants to talk about. Frank did not rob local, which was smart she thought. Then she spent the next minutes trying to reconcile that thought in her mind, with the reality that Frank actually stole people's hard earned money, maybe even killing some folks along the way. She finally let go thinking about it, as the fact is for a robber, it was smart to not rob local, not just, but smart.

They had a buyer within three weeks. $800.00 for four hundred acres. That was fine money and she was pleased with the sale. Maqoom gave her his answer as they were emptying her personal possessions out of the house and onto the wagon that would take her to the train station.

"Mother, I am not going with you, but I am going to

take the money from town to town, trying to make it right."

She smiled, "Well Maqoom, I want to split the farm money half and half with you."

Maqoom insisted though, "Mother $200.00 will be plenty for me and you should take the rest." He really did not want the $200.00, but he knew it pleased her to give him some cash, so he took it, being his desire to see her joyful, grateful and smiling. Contented is how he thought of it. After taking the 200 she looked contented, giving him gratefulness through that. Giving and receiving is not just concerning money he knew. Giving another a dollar is not necessarily the most satisfying for either party. Maqoom received more internal clarity, joy, gratefulness, calmness by taking the money from his mother, than any dollar figure could ever buy. Knowing also within himself, that his mother received about the same within her, because he did take the 200. This receiving was actually a giving, for each of them. He looked up at the blue sky, thinking how amazing God is, that if one is paying attention, one finds out that what he thinks is one way, actually can be that plus another. Outlook, paying attention, contemplation, knowledge of the truth of the Creator, can turn any physical situation into a spiritual exercise of building a relationship with Infinity.

As his mother taught him from the Rabbis, that which is Infinite, dwelling in that which is finite. Only the one, true unlimited God could do that. That is why she named him Maqoom, in English. A transliteration of a Hebrew word meaning "The place." That place where Infinity and the finite meet. Where the unlimited Creator, dwells in the finite created being, known as man. At this juncture, Sarah was more than his mother. She was a fellow spirit, who cooperating with her husband and with the Creator, brought another spirit onto this earth.

"Mother, I want to thank you for all that you taught me and for all that you showed me, by how you lived and conducted yourself."

Water welled in her eyes, as she looked at her son with full cognition that he was a mature, spiritual man, who would strive to conduct himself appropriately before the Creator. No words were necessary, only a shared smile.

He followed her to the train station, waved goodbye, with the two of them having tears, streaming down their cheeks. He stood there looking after the train that took her away, until he could no longer hear the rumble of the metal wheels.

As Maqoom stood there, his mind racing, he realized that on those times when he had seen his dad and Hans come back after being away, it was mostly from the West and occasionally the North. He did not see them every time, but more than a couple. It was always at first light, when he would be out doing his chores. Like they spent the night watching the place, to make sure it was ok to come in, he pondered. Yes, that is probably why. He decided he was going to head West, as that was the direction they came from, this last journey they had. Before he moved, he looked up. The sky was expansive and deep blue. He smiled. Allowing the blueness to take his thoughts towards Heaven and the Creator, his smile broadened.

"Heavenly Father, I am not fully aware of the ramifications before Your Court concerning the killing of humans that I have done. It is written '…shed man's blood, by man shall your blood be shed.' As of this time standing here, to me at this point, it seems it was just, but only You know for sure. Ask You I do, that if I am going to be tempted to go wrong at any time, but before deciding to do so, I think of my dad and on account of him decide to do that which is right; ask You I do, that if I succeed in that decision to do right, that You give the credit for that right act to my dad, as the thought of him inspired me to do right. Maybe to relieve any torment that his soul may be going through. Also, ask I do, to please give him conscious thought that I do not hate him. Amen."

He rode to the farm, stopped to take one last look at the place, from afar. Definitely some memories here, as it was the only place he had ever lived. After brief minutes, he nudged his horse in her sides and reined her West.

Chapter 3
Lessons

The first town he came to, was an eight day ride. He had no idea where he was and it did not really matter to him. As he came into town, he saw there was a sheriff's office and a bank on the opposite side of the street, further along about 80 yards or so. He wanted to know if the local bank had ever been robbed, so he headed to the sheriff's office.

As he entered the sheriff's office, Sheriff Joe was cordial enough, with both greeting one another with mutual, "Hellos".

Maqoom asked, "Has the bank been robbed here in the past?"

Sheriff Joe stated, "The bank was robbed about six weeks back, two men. They rode out blazing, heading South. They got 2200 dollars. People's hard earned money. It has ruined more than one family."

Maqoom stated, "Two men, hmm. Well, I have ran into two men and I have their money. It is my current desire to return the money to the bank, with the hope that those families you speak of, can get back on their feet."

"How did you get the money?" Sheriff Joe asked.

"They both accepted a bullet from me, in exchange for the money."

Sheriff Joe stood up and just stared at him, right in his eyes. Maqoom maintained his stance and sight line, thinking, is he going to draw on me? Maqoom was ready in case it happened, but it was not what he expected.

Finally, the sheriff took a step and said, "Let's go to the bank!"

Maqoom was thankful that the sheriff did not draw on him and Maqoom realized he had a lot to learn about humans. If I cannot trust the sheriff, will I ever be able to trust anyone, other than Mother he thought.

Sheriff Joe introduced him to Mr. Jim Peters, the bank President. Sheriff Joe told Mr. Peters, "This young man wants to return the money those two robbers took some weeks back. All 2200 dollars of it."

Maqoom thought he had made a mistake, as now he does not know if the bank was robbed or not. The sheriff told the bank man how much. Oh well, he was into it now and not going to back out. Another lesson learned he hoped.

The bank man quizzically stated, "He looks kind of young?" Then looking directly at Maqoom he also asked, "How did you come about the money son?"

Maqoom stated that he, "...gave the men some bullets for the money, one apiece!"

2200 dollars was counted out, with the bank man counting it as well. He seemed really grateful to be getting the money and as a crowd somewhat started to form, Maqoom heard whispers of the money being brought back, this giving him some ease as to know there really was a robbery here just some weeks ago. As Maqoom was walking out, he realized this did not go well. Too many people knew about it and are watching and talking about it. Others are already riding out to tell more. *Shucks*, he thought. Put myself in it already, the first town and too many people know what he has done and might want to do at more towns.

There was a fifty dollar reward for that money, which

the bank man counted out for him and he took it. He got some supplies, watered his horse and headed out of town. Maqoom did not want to stay, wanting out of town a ways, well before dark. As the town was disappearing to his rear, he was shaking his head on how naive and stupid he had handled that. Did not even think of a plan before hand, just rode right in and advertised it all. The sun was setting, which he first noticed because of the coolness that he was starting to feel. Without the sun, the air can definitely change temperature. He could feel the heat of the sun on his cheeks and chin, as well as the coolness of the air on the back of his hands and neck. He smiled. The birds were flying overhead, heading to their roosts, noisy as anything. He was grateful that he could sense the heat of the sun, and the cool of the air. His smile broadened as he watched the flocks of birds undulating like a serpent up and down through the air, noisy all the way. *Life*, he thought to himself. He was grateful for life. For the ability to sense all he was sensing and for the comprehension to be aware of it, as well as grateful. He smiled even more as he realized he was grateful to be grateful and lifted his eyes somewhat to see the blue sky, keeping the brim of his hat between his eyes and the sun, mentally thanking the Creator for all this.

Not too long before sunset, he spotted a nice location for camp. It looked like an opening inside a thicket, where it would be hard for people to just walk in on him. Unsaddling his horse, he laid his bedding out, got a fire going, eating a bite all before full dark. What really got his attention was the big limb, running horizontal out from the tree, about 12 foot up off the ground. It was big enough for him to lay on it. The tree was so big, blocking out so much of the sun, was the reason for the somewhat open ground under it. He did not want to lay in his bed roll, knowing he messed up back in town. As his mind was ruminating over the past day's events, he realized he sure has a lot to learn about people and interacting with them. He made the bedding look like someone was under it, putting his hat at the head of it. The fire was burning nicely, of which even after settling in on the limb, with his head towards the trunk, at 20 yards away, he could still feel the heat on his cheek skin. The fire was fairly lined up with the trunk of the tree, so to look squarely at the fire he had to not only turn his head to the left, but slightly tilt his neck back as well. It was not the best shooting angle, but the most comfortable with the limb being so thick near the trunk and somewhat flattened, that he was not concerned much with rolling off. The shooting angle would have to be handled, if that time came. He wanted to get some kind of rest. The limb was not too uncomfortable, nor was it comfortable. Figuring he would get some sleep, before being able to bear it no more, he settled in. It was better to be tired than dead, went through his mind.

The fire was embers, as he was dreaming of chopping wood on the farm, when in his dream a horse let out a soft snort of air. His eyes opened immediately. He did not throw his head to look, but just moved his eyes. His horse stood where he tied it up, its head and neck raised up, head and ears turned towards the sound. Maqoom focused on his own ears. Somewhat opening them as he intentionally, mentally tried to get them to open and focus. The slight brush of limbs on leather, from the direction he came in. Someone's here. Looking out the corner of his left eye, he saw the first shape take form as it stepped into the opening under the tree canopy. The second and third were close behind, one on each side of the first. As they got closer to the bed roll, the ones on each side, spread out slightly, so they were not all bunched up. The first one walked right up to within feet of the bed roll, raised his arm and shot straight into the chest of the bed roll. Not even an attempt to wake him or rough him up and rob him, just straight out murder.

Maqoom, with his left arm, swung his hand over towards the shooter, slightly turning his head to take a partial aim, put the end of the barrel where it should be to catch the shooter in the forehead and pulled the trigger. The bullet caught the shooter just above the left eyebrow, traveling through the brain, blowing out the lower right side and at such an angle that it caught his shoulder as well, embedding within it, thereby jerking the shooters body to the right slightly, as it went immediately limp otherwise. Before the shooter's body fully rested on the ground, Maqoom was already in motion on the farthest one away, as he appeared to be the most ready of the two remaining. As his armed hand went for the intruder, he raised his torso also, to get a better angle on the man, making sure his feet did not drop below the bottom of the limb, which the movement would be easily seen, as the vertical feet hanging in open air, would be in full contrast compared to the background of a horizontal dark limb. Maqoom aimed for the bridge of his nose but caught him right between his nostril and upper cheek bone. Maqoom actually thought he heard the crushing of bone as the bullet ripped into his cheek, busting loose the upper jawbone, existing just below the left ear, behind the lower jawbone. The man went down hard, having enough reflexes within him to bring his left hand up to his cheek before he fell too far to the ground. Just as Maqoom was swinging on the third man, the closet man, the man had his pistol drawn and was raising it up. Before the man got the gun pointed at Maqoom, the man fired off his first shot. The bullet caught the tree below the limb where Maqoom was perched. He fired too early. Maqoom did not let him fire twice. Maqoom's bullet caught the man squarely in his left eye, bulging out the other eye, traveling through the brain before breaking out the lower right skull and hitting the ground with a thud. Within what was no more than four seconds from the first shot, all three were at full rest.

Maqoom remained still in case there were others. He wanted to get the bodies over their horses before they got stiff, but he did not want to move until being more confident there were no more. He put his pistol on his chest, actually falling asleep for a spell. When his eyes opened, it must have been because of the chill he was feeling, as he was not terribly uncomfortable. The fire had completely gone out, but his night vision was in full effect. All three bodies laid where they rested. He got down on the ground, finding their horses, bringing them to the bodies. The men were bigger than him and their corpses already stiffened up. It would be hours before their bodies would start to go limp again, and he did not want to wait. Chopping wood, lifting lumber and fighting cows that wanted to go another way helped tone him up, but he knew he did not have his full man muscles yet. The horses were well trained and not body shy, as once he got a body against the saddle, he would grab it around the upper legs, below the hip bones, lift and slide the body over the saddle, thereby not having to try to lift its whole weight. The stiffness helped actually, as the upper torso did not bend as he lifted, but it did not help the body lay in the saddle appropriately. He had to not push too hard, as the body would slide off on the other side, since the corpses did not yet lay limp, taking the shape of the saddle. That is what he was thinking at first, to get them on their saddles and let them stiffen in that position. Because they were already stiff, this meant he had to tie them somewhat more securely than would have been necessary otherwise. The horse's weight and still stance allowed Maqoom's exertion to push the body up and over, sliding across the saddle and into position. The heaviest of the three though, he tied a rope to him, threw the rope over a high limb and used another horse, that already had a body on it, to get this third body in the air. He then walked the horse that was going to carry the man under him, drove the other horse backward to let the man come to full rest. The horses were calm and cooperative, he was grateful for that. Eventually gravity and returning limpness would allow the bodies to arch over the saddle, helping them to remain in place. Maqoom did not want to disrespect the body, nor did he want to have to pick them up again, especially limp, now that he realized his original thinking was wrong. With the work done and daylight breaking, he realized he did not say thank you through the whole ordeal. He looked East, just before any direct beam of the sun would hit him, looked up a bit into the sky, verbally saying out loud, "Thank You!"

He came back into town, holding the reigns of one horse with the other two, each tied behind the other. He rode straight to the sheriff's office, tying his own horse off at the post.

Sheriff Joe opened the door to greet him. "Morning young man!"

"Morning sheriff! These three men, I believe, wanted to see if I had any more money on me. One of them I recognize from yesterday at the bank. The other two I do not. This first one walked straight up to my bed roll and shot it straight in the chest without even attempting to converse. Thankfully, I was not in the bedroll, which brings us to now."

Sheriff Joe looked over all three, asking Maqoom, "Do you always shoot for the face?"

Maqoom answered, "The position and angle called for it."

The man Maqoom recognized, the sheriff knew as well. Sheriff Joe shared, "This one is a local, no real trouble maker, just when he got drunk. Spent a night or two in jail sleeping it off. The other two are strangers to me, but one looks like a wanted poster that I have." Sheriff Joe went in the jail, coming back out with a poster. Grabbed the man's hair on the back of his head, lifting his face. "Yep, that is him. It seems like money flows right to you young man, like heat rising from the earth. This man is worth another fifty to you. That is fifty a day for two days straight. Some men work a whole year just to see slightly half of what you made in two days. The way money flows to you, so too will men, looking for a fast buck."

Sheriff Joe got the fifty and counted it out to Maqoom.

Maqoom then asked, "How much will it cost to bury the men? As I do not want the town to have to pay for that."

Sheriff Joe stated, "a buck fifty will cover all three."

Maqoom gave him two, told him "Thank you," got on his horse and headed out of town for the second time in two days.

Just as Maqoom was getting on his horse, Sheriff Joe said, "Young man, you must be real fine with those weapons. That is three that I know of you killed, as well as the two bank robbers, making five total. Keep this up and you will have killed more men than your age."

Maqoom paused, "It is not my desire sheriff. It is my desire to do what is right. Some men just refuse to let that happen, like it bothers them or something. It is the easier road to do evil, when surrounded by it. One has to work to do right, when in the midst of evil. The only thing I really have in life – is to strive to live right." Maqoom did not look back. He trusted Sheriff Joe not to shoot him in the back. Thankfully that trust paid off, as the town was behind him for the second time, with no bullet catching him from behind. Maqoom pondered that for a long time, as he rode. Why would he turn his back to the sheriff and ride out of town? He had no idea if the sheriff would draw and shoot him. It is just the way he did it, he did not have an answer as to why; eventually letting go of mentally wrestling with it. He knew he had to try to be more careful and smarter. He was thankful to be alive, and looked up at the big blue sky, smiling, while giving out another verbal, "Thank You!"

He also apologized, while looking up, for his carelessness in trusting Sheriff Joe so much. He knew it was his responsibility to strive to stay alive, to do his part and then trust for the Creator's Will to be done. After pondering it, he realized within himself that he wanted the sheriff to know that another human trusted him. He wanted to give that to the sheriff, like a gift. He did not want to falsely accuse the sheriff of wanting to kill him and he does not want to be careless neither. So, the lesser of the two evils so to speak, was to show Sheriff Joe he trusted him, thereby giving to the sheriff the sense that someone trusts him. It was very important to Maqoom to give to his fellow humans and not embarrass them in any way, if at all possible. He looked up at that big blue sky again, smiling broadly with true joy within him. Maqoom also had a strong sense to give to the Creator, but the Creator is everything, lacking nothing. So a thank you when appropriate and a sincere smile was at least giving

Maqoom the sense that he was giving something to show his own appreciation for everything the Creator was doing for him. That thought made his smile broaden more and he gave another out loud, "Thank You!"

Chapter 4
Lessons Applied

Maqoom had it much smoother in the next town. He rode in, got a room, took a hot bath and donned clean clothes. He had a nice, hot home cooked meal at the hotel. Visited the local paper office the next day, discovering there was $2500.00 stolen by two men, back two years ago. He stayed in town one more night, getting rested up and filled up on such delicious food. That night after his meal, he took a walk, looking up with the whole sky totally clear. The coolness of the evening was settling down, he could feel it on his cheeks, as he looked skyward. He said thanks again for his meal and to be able to experience such clean, calm living conditions, as he had for the past day. More stars than he could count filled the night sky. He smiled. Such grandeur he thought, and the Creator made it all. His smile broadened as he closed his eyes and focused on the awesomeness of God.

After a sound, refreshing night's sleep, first thing in the morning Maqoom visited the bank. He spoke with the bank President, informing him why he was there, "…To return the money, hopefully to the rightful owners."

$2500.00 was counted out, with a $50.00 dollar reward going back to Maqoom. The bank man said "thank you," of which Maqoom acknowledged and was out the door.

Smooth and simple. No one aware except the bank

man, for the moment, with no one following him, nor Maqoom expecting any one to do so. Maqoom was pleased that no one else knew, as they would not be tempted to track him, seeing if he had more. That meant lives spared, either theirs or his. Maqoom was pleased with that. While in the paper office, there was a story of a bank losing $5000.00 to two men, approximately 15 days ride, due West. Maqoom's next destination.

Chapter 5
The Beast

I t was the ninth morning out from the last town. Oh, what a morning. Before he could fully decipher that dawn was approaching, the birds were already stirring, with some commencing their morning vocals. As the first hint of yellow appeared on the horizon, it was a full symphony, of what seemed to Maqoom, harmonious sound. The air fresh, with the morning breeze being cool as it silently caressed his cheeks, with the first morning crack of the sun, already producing heat upon his skin. He turned his face, to get the cool brush of breeze on his one cheek and the heat of the sun on the other. His smile broadened and he looked up, blessing the Creator for such auditory and visual beauty, as well as for his senses. For the ability to pick out and appreciate the differing, what seemed opposite, but yet, what is all part of one point in time, one congruous flow of life. So much input from so many various sources and directions, yet all one. The vocals, smells, visual, feeling, the sixth sense of the spirit within him, all brought together within his mind, his being, pointing to God. He suddenly realized he had his eyes closed, instantly they opened, being much later than he intended, but with no regrets. He had just communed with his Creator. That interface, that place within, where Infinity meets the finite, having no other comparison on earth, nor within all of creation, he knew he lost nothing and gained everything.

It was midday, with his stomach telling him it was time to eat. As he looked for a spot to rest and eat, he had the first sight of what made him sit up straight, with back arched and with ears stretched back, trying to make them spread out to help catch any hint of a whisper of a sound that may give him an indication of danger. With suddenness, his leisurely ride became quite tense. The wagon trail he was on went straight, except for a slight left leaning. But to the right, was a trail, that was much clearer. On each side of the trail where two posts, with a human skull on top of each of them. He stopped his horse, watching and listening. Not much noise at midday, a bird fluttering here or there, but mostly quiet. He sat probably five minutes or so, hearing nothing out of the ordinary nor picking up on any sense that would give him the impression he was being watched. Prodding his horse on, he rode up to the posts, stopping to inspect the heads. One was all bone, but the other still had some flesh in places on it. Some insects and fly's still working on the last pieces. The wagon trail before him contained a slight incline, so he could not see over it, even sitting on the horse. Suddenly, a woman's scream, just a horrible shrill of fear. The hair on the back of his neck stood up, with even the horse jerking slightly, as it faced forward with both ears pointing like directional signs straight ahead. The scream came again, with such intensity, it almost made his body shudder. Maqoom wanted to ride in to see if he could help, but to burst into this situation, may be his last decision on earth, so he forced himself to pause.

Maqoom nudged the horse forward, whom, without Maqoom holding the horse back, went at its own slow pace, being vigilant with its eyes and ears. Up the incline they went until Maqoom could see over the lip. It was not so steep as to prevent him from seeing the whole other side, as soon as his eyes cleared the rise. He pulled the horse to a stop. Five poles in an opening, at the end of the trail. Four of them had humans in front of them. As he focused, he realized they were all women. There was a house off to the left of the women, which he could make out bits and pieces of it through the trees.

Dismounting, he walked over the knoll leading his horse. His rifle had been in his hand since the first scream. About 20 yards from the clearing, he halted and tied the reins, lightly to a tree limb. The horse could pull it loose, if necessary. The women had spotted him, almost looking astonished that there was another human on the planet. So hoping was he that they would stay silent, so far they had. One or two of them caught a glimpse of him as he cleared the knoll, but now all four knew of his presence. They all were tied to the posts. Instead of their hands by their sides, they were back behind them. Not drastically, but enough they could not get them past their midpoint.

He was thankful, for what the Creator did for him earlier that morning. Had the morning meeting been in preparation for this? He wanted to live, but whether he lived or died, he was fully engaged in accepting the Divine Will. After leaving the horse he walked to the far side of the trail, away from the house. On that corner was a huge oak tree, that he easily could completely disappear behind. He cleared the far side of the tree, just enough to be able to see the whole house, off to his left, with the tree blocking most of his body, or at least he would look like a part of the tree on the base. Looking at the women, they all had wide eyed stares, like they were pleading with him for something. Thankfully, no one uttered a word. He fixed his gaze somewhat straight ahead, between two of the posts, slightly angled down, so as to be looking at the earth, yet with peripheral vision fully able to notice movement anywhere his eyes allowed him to perceive. Maqoom was fixed in his intent to be fully conscious of what was happening around him. Eyes focused, head not moving, so any movement he would notice. Ears stretched back in an effort to open up the channels leading into the eardrums. His whole body engaged in striving to pick up any signal whatsoever that could mean the difference between life or death. His brain was working so hard to remain blank as possible to focus on the situation at hand. Processing vision, sound, smell, any vibration felt by his feet or skin. Quickly he perceived that a slight breeze was blowing across his left, coming from the house past him; of which he was thankful, that it was not blowing his scent toward the house. He did not know how he smelled, nor what he was dealing with, nor how many.

A creak, the door opened, a foot protruding out from the bowels of the house to the outside air, for the covered porch floor. As the remaining part of the leg and body followed that was attached to that foot, even in his peripheral vision, he could sense his own eyes widening at the size of what was stepping from inside the house. Maqoom, slightly twisted his head, just enough to allow both eyes to focus on the being. A huge man, easily over 7 foot tall, with Maqoom judging him to be eight. No shirt, which allowed for the view of the full upper body, exposing muscles that bulged on this person. Bare foot with just pants on, that ended just below the knees. In his right hand he held a woman, under her left armpit. She looked completely unconscious as she was completely limp, being dragged across the wood planks, touching them from her knees down. There were four steps to go down from the porch, which as the being traversed them, the woman's knees and feet would klump twice on each step. Klump, klump, klump, klump down the four until her feet landed on the ground. What by now Maqoom considered a beast, took maybe three more steps, each easily over three feet, raised his right arm out away from his midpoint, lifting the women up to about his waist height and letting her go. The toss took her body out approximately two more feet, with gravity pushing her down, as she hit the dry, dusty earth with a slight thud. Dust stirred up slightly, all around her upper portion, then settling. The beast was not intently concerned about something being amiss in his yard, but was engaged in monitoring the situation, as Maqoom could see his nostrils flare as it was checking the breeze, with Maqoom now being very grateful for the direction of it.

It was not Maqoom's makeup to let situations ride out, to see what would happen, so he tightened his grip on the rifle, which was in his right hand, taking one step out from behind the tree, fully exposing himself to the beast. Without warning, nor even appearing to look first, the beast was in motion, charging like a bull, but with the speed of a mountain lion. The approximate 80 yards disappeared even faster than Maqoom imagined, with huge leaps that made it appear as if the beast had no friction with the earth whatsoever. With half the distance already gone, before Maqoom even made another move, he raised the rifle, judging to put the bullet directly in the left eye of the man. The gun roared, with the beast still coming, showing no slowness. The beast had read him. Even coming as fast and intently as it was, it was as if the beast was fully aware of Maqoom's placement and actions, knowing to move his head slightly to the right, just as Maqoom pulled the trigger. The lever of the gun was worked without thought, being made ready to fire again. Maqoom knew not to look at the man, but kept his eyesight, slightly lowered, gun halfway up, as if he was in a state of shock, not fully grasping what just happened. The beast was already in the air, feet off the ground, as it made the last yards coming at Maqoom like a body bullet. His arms were already stretched out, hands fully open ready to grasp Maqoom and do what Maqoom did not want to know. Maqoom was still showing signs of shock, as the beast's hands were coming inward for the grasp. Now! Maqoom thought. He raised the rifle just enough to line up with the left eye of the beast. His rifle and arms slightly outstretched, still did not match the length of the creature's grasp, so just as the beast's hands were going to grasp him, he jutted the rifle out a couple more inches, pulling the trigger. The left eye of the beast was on a collision course with the end of Maqoom's rifle barrel. By the time the bullet cleared the barrel, the eye and barrel may already have been touching. The bullet entering directly into the beast's pupil and blowing out the back of the head. The skull being so thick, making the bullet expansively mushroom out, forcing its exit. Smashing and cracking skull, as it forcefully pushed its way through. Maqoom actually caught a glimpse of brain matter blowing out the back of the skull, following the bullets exit.

There was no time to move, but to relax, hoping to just take a glancing blow from the airborne body. The bullet's exit caused the beast to lose forward momentum, as the stiffness of the attack was being replaced with the passivity of death. Gravity almost instantaneously pushing down the body of the beast, with its left shoulder catching Maqoom in a glancing blow across his left ribs. Even though it was not a direct blow, the impact pushed Maqoom through the air, with him landing a good five feet from where he was. Almost immediately he felt the pain in his rib area, but that was not his first concern at this moment. Was the beast going to get up? As Maqoom hit the ground, he was mechanically racking another round in the chamber. Maqoom swung his feet around to his right, with such force that he was right where he wanted, on his knees with the rifle ready. The pain that speared from his ribs to his brain almost made his eyes close, but he had to keep his attention on the beast. Finally hearing his own breathing, as he was taking huge, quick successive amounts of air through his nostrils, he realized the beast was not moving and he worked to calm himself down, getting back to paying attention, if anything else was closing in on him. Taking a quick, half circle look to this left then his right, he was at least assured nothing was closing in on him at this point. He was not looking to get close to the beast at this juncture, as even in death a muscle reflex could kill a normal human. He kept vigilance of his surroundings, making his way to one of the women.

Chapter 6
Freedom

His brain picked up on the blue sky his eyes were sending along his nerves. He looked up and with his lips, said, "Thank You!"

Staying just outside of her reach, in case her hands were not fully tied, he asked, "Are there any more?"

She was just staring at him, making no movement. He asked a second time, in a calmer tone, resulting this time with the woman shaking her head back and forth, visually replying no.

He wanted to cut their ropes but had no idea if they would immediately attack him or what they would do, so he was patient. He went to the woman on the end, closest to the house asking the same question.

This time a verbal response came back, "No, he is the only one I have ever seen."

Now also, the first woman, who gave the head shake verbalized it as well, "No, I have been here the longest and he is the only one I have ever seen as well."

Maqoom took his knife out, cutting the ropes of each one, successively down the line. They helped each other get the ropes off their wrists. The one who had been a captive of the beast the longest, turned to Maqoom stating, "I cannot believe what just happened. Other men had come, with the beast ripping them to pieces with his bare hands. They would shoot, but miss too, just like your first shot did."

With that Maqoom looked at the beast, as its left side was facing up, and there on the ear was a small spot of blood. He moved closer, realizing that a piece of ear was missing, but it was not even the thickness of the bullet, that which was gone. Maqoom was impressed with what senses and perception this man-beast was given. It was his intent to let the beast lay there for a spell before going over to it, but before he could finish that thought, one of the women was already racing towards the beast, dropping her knees square on its back and punching it with her fists, screaming at the lifeless being.

One of the women volunteered that in her town, "They spoke of the beast harassing people for generations and they called it a man-beast."

Maqoom spoke then saying, "Humanoid."

A couple of the ladies looked at him, with one verbalizing their community thought, "Humanoid?"

Maqoom stated, "It has been a question of mine, that I have wondered in the past, if Noah had any humanoids on the ark. Man creatures, created, but like any other beast, who did not have the Breath of Life, from the Creator breathed into them. Well, this answers my question. Do not like seeing the total destruction of any creature's kind, but man and this humanoid are definitely not compatible." Maqoom was sadly, glad to be useful, in removing another one from the earth, as a lot of lives would be spared with its end.

Maqoom's ribs hurt. As best as he could tell, none were broken, but maybe cracked and definitely highly bruised. Two of the women, aware that the beast made contact, also noticing Maqoom checking himself out, volunteered to wrap his ribs with a torn sheet. Maqoom accepted, with the ladies wrapping his ribs nice and tight, tucking the tip snugly in the fold to hold. Before he could get his shirt back on, one of them stated, "You're just a boy! How old are you?"

Maqoom did not answer. He did not know if he should or not, so he stayed silent on the question, continuing his current endeavors, asking a question of his own. "There are no others here but you four?"

"That is correct," came the reply.

Maqoom checked the barn, where he found a stockpile of various weapons. Rifles, pistols, knives, almost as many as any hardware store he had ever been in. There was a large wagon with two of the biggest horses he had ever seen standing in their stalls, looking directly at him with their big ears facing his direction. They did not seem scared in the least, and allowed him to draw close to them, running his fingers through their manes and stroking their necks, each one in turn. On his way to the barn, he noticed some cows, and another horse down the slope, in a pasture to the right of the barn. So he had the wagon and the horses to haul the beast to town, but how to get the creature into the wagon, that was the current question.

Three of the ladies were aghast, when they realized what he was contemplating, taking the beast back to town. They wanted out of there immediately. Maqoom told them, "You are free to leave anytime you like, I am not holding any of you here." None departed the premises.

Maqoom hitched up one of the horses to the wagon, walking it out under the same huge oak tree that he was sheltering behind at the beginning of this endeavor. There was a limb, not to high, but higher than the tall horse that Maqoom wanted to use as a lift, by throwing a heavy rope over the limb and utilizing the horses to pull the beast up and onto the wagon. The wagon he pulled slightly past the limb, then unhitched the horse from it. Both horses, he then put into the wagon's dual harness system. Thankfully, there was plenty of large, long ropes in the barn, of which he hung one rope over the limb, and out past the wagon for another 50 feet or so. Another rope, with the help of all four women, he got in place under the armpits of the beast and tied a tight knot in the rope, with the knot, on the chest side of the beast. It took all five of them to roll the beast over, with it not being an easy roll. The rope was in place before rolling the beast, with three of them getting the tag end and pulling it under the beast to get enough to tie off. This was tied to the horse team, who thankfully showed no concern or fear that their master was dead. The team pulled the body across the ground and into position for the second phase. With the body lined up, Maqoom tied the two tag ends from the two separate ropes together. Then leading the horses to the other side of the wagon, he tied the rope securely to the midpoint of the harness. Then coaxing the horses forward, the beast's body started to drag forward and up. As half the beast was in the air, the horses started to really have to pull then. They pushed their heads forward, pressing their weight into their feet, straining their bodies and the rope. The rope was sliding over the limb, showing no visible nor audible signs of breaking, with the limb holding steady as well. When the head of the beast was touching the limb, Maqoom ordered the women to push the wagon backwards, so that the middle of the wagon was under the humanoid. With this accomplished, Maqoom started to walk the horses backward, slowly while two women, each pulled a foot of the humanoid towards the back of the wagon. With the humanoid centered over the wagon, and the heels of the beast where Maqoom wanted them, he allowed the horses to let down the beast the rest of the way, until it laid somewhat squarely in the wagon bed. Maqoom smiled at the success of the endeavor, with the women appearing somewhat pleased as well, with Maqoom looking up at the blue sky and verbalizing, "Thank You!" My how he liked these horses. So big, yet so gentle and human friendly. They deserve nice homes, of which he was hoping to make sure that happened.

He asked the women to load up the weapons and cover the beast with a blanket or two or three, so none of it was exposed. It was well past midday, with him realizing that he had not eaten and was hungry. He did not have enough on his saddle pack to feed all of them, but they knew where the food was, vegetables and some dried beef, that they took care of themselves, even offering him some greens, which he accepted gratefully. Not wanting to stay any longer than necessary, but not wanting to leave and be stuck without a camp, he pondered the situation. Before he fully decided whether to leave immediately or stay until morning, one of the women stated, "There is something odd, that you may want to look into."

Chapter 7
The Pet

Maqoom turned to look at her, not verbalizing anything, but waiting for her to continue. She did. "There were times that some men were captured alive and the beast would walk them to the west side of the house, opposite where their posts were, only being gone for mere minutes, always coming back without them. Even when they were not tied, allowed to roam the yard doing their chores, they never went on that side of the house for more than a mere glimpse to see what might be there."

Well, that settles that he thought. "We are staying the night," he verbalized.

After a light meal, Maqoom took a chair off the porch, setting it at the southwest corner of the house. The ladies were content, in their new found freedom. Each able to do what she wanted to do, sit where she wanted to sit, take a walk or just sit and think. To be able to make their own decisions, as to what they wanted to do or where they wanted to go, improved their personal dispositions drastically.

In front of Maqoom was a slightly worn path, not really perceptible unless looking for it. At the entrance of the tree line was a path, approximately as wide as a cow, proceeding into the trees approximately ten feet, ending at an opening, oval in shape as best as he could tell. The opening seemed to be ten to twelve feet at its widest.

Maqoom looked, listened and thought. Darkness was mostly upon them, when Maqoom got up from his chair, to get some rest. The ladies went into the house, Maqoom went to the barn. Earlier he had put both of the big horses in their stalls with food and water, also stalling his horse as well. In the stall beside his horse is where he would sleep. He trusted the instincts of his horse, so if anything strange was coming through the door, he believed his horse's nervousness would wake him. The hay was soft and his saddle blanket helped to keep his body heat in. The roof of the barn keeping the night chilled air off of him, as it fell. Being so comfortable, he slept well past his normal. Usually, awake with the first morning birds, as they start their new day songs. Some species, singing well before most humans could perceive that the sun is coming up. The barn walls helped too, as it muffled the sound of the birds. First light was cracking the horizon and he had to pay attention to notice the birds. First thing he wanted to do was get to the southwest corner of the house. As he was going past the porch, one of the ladies came out and handed him a cup of hot coffee. He accepted, saying "thank you."

At the corner he watched and listened. There was something noticeable, as he picked up no bird movement in that location, as well as there was almost no bird song coming from that direction. He picked his head up, stretching his ears back and using his mind to pay attention. Definitely, there was sound from all around him, but not in front of him. Something was there he thought, but why does it not come out, if it is hungry?

Before he decided to move, he perceived something coming towards him from the right rear. Turning, it was one of the ladies with fried onions and potatoes, with two eggs too. Wow he thought. A meal for a king. He accepted, thanking her twice, verbalized the blessing over the provided food, then sat down in his chair to eat the meal and watch. A minute later, another lady was refilling his coffee cup. "Thank you" he stated. What a meal he thought as he looked up and gave his thanks for such bounty. Having made his decision on what he was going to do, he stood, passing the porch where all four were sitting and talking after finishing their own plates. He asked, "May I leave this plate and cup on the porch?

The ladies gave an affirmative response of, "Yes, we'll take care of it."

He thanked them all, then moved on.

Maqoom headed to the lower field where he noticed some other horses and cows the day before. Looking over the livestock, he noticed a very big bull standing under a tree at the edge of the far woods. He came closer to it, ever vigilant of the bull's disposition, as it could charge without notice. Earlier, he fashioned a rope halter, which he now slipped on the bull, with no dissatisfaction being shown by the bull whatsoever. Having a couple ears of corn, which he let the bull smell, he started walking with the bull leisurely coming along. Around the house he went, clearing the southwest corner, walking towards the opening. The ladies followed, but they did not go past the corner of the house.

Approximately 10 yards from the path in the trees, he took the corn ears and tossed them into the clearing, with both landing on the far side. Continuing with the bull, he allowed his feet to stop, but kept the forward pressure on the harness. As the bull walked away from him towards the corn, he opened his hand, allowing the harness to slip out of his grasp as the bull moved forward. Thereby preventing any backward pressure on the harness. The bull walked.

This was a big bull, with Maqoom guessing it easily went over 800 pounds. His dad had one or two that pushed 400, and this one was twice the girth of them. He had a pang of guilt creep into his conscience, as the bull walked forward. Such a gentle, trusting creature he thought. Knowing the bull could easily kill man and beast alike with is weight, horns and hooves, yet still the pang of guilt was there. He did not know what was going to happen. As the bull lowered his head to pick up the first ear of corn, there was a flash of movement so fast, that Maqoom did not hear or see anything before contact was made with the bull. The only perceptible inkling of something happening, was a dull brownish flash, like a dust cloud would make in a tornado. That movement was the dull brownish body of what was now riding the bulls back. Both the hands and feet had claws, that even though the length was obscured from his view, he knew they were large and sharp.

Upon impact, the bull's body tightened as the claws sliced through its hide and into its flesh. It gave out a bellow that made Maqoom's own body, involuntarily jerk and tense itself. The bull was mad dashing to the right, away from the point of approach of the thing that had pinned itself to him. As it turned, Maqoom caught sight of the thing, opening its mouth and sinking what looked like four inch canines into the top of its neck. The thing jerked its head viciously to one side, ripping a hunk of flesh out of the top of the neck, what looked like the size of a large man's head. Blood flowed forth, with the cow giving another shuddering bellow, that made Maqoom's body twitch inside. What power and strength, along with such viciousness. A man would not stand a chance.

Then, what looked like a brown rope, maybe eight inches in diameter rose off the ground coming taut, as the bull and beast reached its length limit. This tautness caused the bulls forward progress to come to a complete, almost instant halt. It was with such suddenness and force, that forward momentum of the bull, along with its weight and the weight of the creature on its back, caused its legs to instantly collapse from under it. The thing was ripping another hunk of flesh from the back of the bull's neck, never losing any noticeable grip of the bull, as the forward progress was completely halted. Now however, Maqoom could clearly see the tail of this thing. Maqoom instantly wanted to see the other end of that tail. He knew where the bull was when it came taut, and he wanted to know how far back it went and why did it not follow.

Maqoom raced to his left, trying to keep sight of the taut tail. After what appeared like forever, but was mere seconds, he spotted the end of it, as it sank down into the earth. It looked like an overly large grape vine lying across the ground, with a downward arch at its end, but it definitely went into the ground; like a root he thought to himself. Deep and solid enough that the thing could not pull it out. Easily he had traversed twenty foot, so with the approximate twelve foot wide clearing, he quickly estimated an area of thirty two feet, plus adding a couple feet for possible miscalculations, roughly estimating thirty five feet. Instantly he realized he was too close to the root's entrance in the ground.

The motion was not lost to the creature. As busy as it was with the bull, it knew Maqoom was within his domain. One more rip at the bull's neck and it was not going anywhere. As Maqoom was making his realization that he was to close, the thing was making its way to Maqoom, with the speed of a big cat, actually faster than a cat. Because it could not go straight for Maqoom because of two large trees that its root was on the wrong side of, it had to go past those trees before making a bee line to Maqoom. Saplings, brush, limbs anything in its way just bent or broke as it speeded towards Maqoom. Maqoom, thinking he was at least forty feet from the root, spun around to face the beast, just as the claws of the thing reached out for him. Maqoom had no comprehension that the thing could make such speed. Having it right in front of him so close, so unexpectedly, made him jerk his head back, although it would have been a useless gesture, if he was not clear of those claws. Sensing it was not enough, the thing stretched against his root tail, striving to get those bloody claws into Maqoom's face. To no avail, it was not enough. Twelve more inches, maybe less and Maqoom would be dying or dead already. The thing was straining to gain that small space, Maqoom heard creaking like wood under heavy strain. The claws looked six inches long, covered in blood with pieces of meat from the bull still attached. Thick, heavy and pointed. Arched on top, with a slight inward arch, on the underside, so that there were two razor edges, one on each side on the underside of them. The mouth was huge, with definitely four inch canines and a mouth full of what appeared to be slicing teeth, with the top ones diamond shaped, fitting nicely into the reverse diamond shaped ones on the bottom. Maqoom had to do something now. He did not want to have to figure out how to get this thing later, after it gets back hiding in its foliage lair. Without much conscious thought, he took a large step back, pulling out both pistols from their holsters, jutting them forward to almost touching the claws. One pointed at each eyeball, with both going off almost simultaneously. The creature's arms were pushing four feet, so the bullets only had to travel about five feet to find their marks. Both bullets hit where intended. The things skin was tough, almost like bark, but not quite. More like what possibly an elephant's hide would be, as he read of them before. The eyes, as with everything about this thing were not delicate, but tough. Tough as they were though, they could not, nor did they stop the bullets from entering. The bullets did not come out the back of the head, but they both penetrated deep inside, with an instant rush of fluid coming forth from both eyes. The scream that came out of the creature made him forget about the bull's bellow. This scream was like that of a woman, but what was perceived by Maqoom to be a twenty foot tall woman, with a very high pitched voice, screaming at the top of her lungs. It made Maqoom want to turn and run, his whole body was quivering, with his breathing involuntarily pausing; but he had to stay. This had to be finished, as he could not let this thing live any longer, for unaware passersby to be devoured by it. His breathing commenced again, his body stopped quivering and he shot, again and again, for a total of four bullets in each of its eyes.

The beast dropped to the ground, face first. Its arms outstretched, with its claws pressing down into the earth. Maqoom knew it was not dead. He raced to the barn, where he remembered seeing a large axe. His normal is about three quarters of a pound, but this one must be ten pounds. He was so full of the chemicals that race through one's body, that as he grasped the handle of the axe to pick it up, it raised much easier than he expected it to. Running back to the beast, he fixed his eyes on the center point of the back of the beast's head. Raising the axe, high as he could, Maqoom, aided by gravity, with as much force as he could muster, sank the axe into the back of the skull of the beast. Kthunk, was the sound as the axe pressed forward through the meat of the skull. Fluid raced out, amber in color. It was not nauseating to him, as it had no mental semblance of blood, but was of the consistency of blood, being somewhere between pine sap and water. Not too thick, not to thin. The beast's extremities went rigid, then with one last violent shudder, the beast relaxed its hold upon the earth, with the claws no longer pressing down.

Maqoom realized that his heart was beating so hard, it was actually moving the top part of his body, waving it back and forth. As he looked at the trees, they were still, but his eyes were moving ever so slightly, back and forth as his head and upper torso were being jerked, by the force of his heart beating, pumping the blood forth. His breaths were almost out of control, so he mentally took in as big of a breath as he could, through his nostrils, filling the lungs as far down as his diaphragm could pull it. Then letting it out, through pursed lips, very slowly, using back pressure to force the air down farther into the lungs, he could sense an almost immediate release of the tenseness within his being. Maqoom thought though that he had to keep the momentum going, while he was worked up. So, he grabbed the axe handle, he got the axe out of the back of the head and raced towards where the root went into the ground, not fully confident within himself if the beast was even indeed dead yet or not. Clearing enough brush, to swing safely, he started to cut that root. He did not know if some huge creature was going to come up out of the earth, swallowing him whole or what, but he was cutting that root. The same amber fluid was running as he cut, splatting him on the cheeks as he went. Hit after hit, cut after cut, finally the last swing and the root was severed. The stump, ever so slightly swinging straight as it was released from the weight of the beast. Maqoom stood, looked up, his heart racing, pounding in his ears, his breaths being huge gasps of air. Through the tree tops he peered, the sky blue with pure white fluffy clouds floating by here and there. He thought of his Creator. Taking some more breaths through his nostrils and forcing them out his pursed lips, he gained some respite from the situation, still looking up, he said out loud, "Thank You!"

Paying attention with his ears and other senses, he gained cognizance, even with all the exertion and concentration he was doing and utilizing to kill this creature, he was alert and aware of his surroundings. Nothing else was coming for him to do harm. Even as he stood looking up, smiling, still breathing hard, heart continuing to settle to normal somewhat, he said thank You over and over, until realizing he could not really say it enough times, he said it again and stopped. Still gazing at the most beautiful blue he thinks he has ever seen. The sense of gratefulness within him, was almost overpowering. He actually perceived the concept that his soul may just jump right out of his body and that would be that. His body would fall to the earth like the beast's. Realizing that this is possible and realizing that if the Creator wanted to take him, it would be done without his assistance, he looked down, straight ahead, closed his eyes and listened. All the while though, giving mental thanks to the Throne of Heaven. He realized also that he should not have his eyes closed, as it was one of the senses the Creator gave him to utilize, so he should. He opened them immediately. He stood silent, listening, watching, hearing, feeling with his skin. Paying attention also to the soul sense within him. He wanted to cling to the connection that he had at this moment with the Divine, at this place. Oh, he wanted to look up, he could sense within him the desire he had to let his soul fly, to be free. Connected to the Divine without the filtering mask of physicality. So one with the Divine, so connected, it would be to the point of silence.

Maqoom smiled so broadly, turned away from the beast, heading to the wagon and the ropes. He was taking the beast with them too. As he turned, his hurt ribs let him know that he abused them again. Grimacing and placing his elbow and forearm against them, he moved forward.

Getting the rope, he headed back to the beast. As he walked by the house, the ladies were all back out at the corner watching. He asked for some help, not speaking directly to any of them, looking for volunteers. Two went behind him, following up to the beast, but stopping at a reasonable distance. Maqoom asked them to grab the beast's arm and help roll it so he could get the rope under its chest. They would not touch it. So, he tied a rope to the arm, handing them the tag end. With them pulling and him pushing up and against it, they got it on its side. Pushing the rope under as far as he could, then allowing the beast to lay back down, he did the same to the other side, but just enough to get the tag end of the rope. Pulling it out enough to tie it tight, he went to get a horse.

The ladies asked, "What is it?"

"From my readings, it is a Yedua, a man of the field, so to speak. A human form but tied to the earth via a root of sorts. There are various written descriptions of what they could look like, not necessarily all of them looking like this one. One characteristic they all share though is viciousness. Wondered I have in the past if there were any still on earth, or if Noah had any on the ark. They could have survived the Great flood by being pods deep in the earth, dormant until their time. Maybe other ways too, that I am not aware of. Now we know they did exist though and may still be somewhere. However, with the expanse of man around the globe, they will get wiped out eventually, being relegated to myth."

Not sure how the horse would respond to this creature, who he was sure it was not accustomed to, he talked to the horse the whole time, walking it up slowly to the creature. Not having to go very close, as the rope was long, the horse gave no bother to the situation, cooperating fully. The same was done to the beast, as with the humanoid, up over the limb and onto the wagon. The big root of a tail was a situation, but working diligently, he got it wound up within the body of the wagon, so he could cover the beast and the humanoid completely. The humanoid was already starting to stink, so it was time to head out at first light. The ladies were ready, with none of them wanting to keep the place as their own.

Maqoom went back to look over the big, trusting, gentle bull. There was guilt within his chest, as to what he caused to happen to this gentle giant of an animal. Less than two hours ago, standing in the shade of a tree, chewing its cud, not a care in the world. Now dead, basically ripped to pieces by another giant, not so gentle. Maqoom mentally apologized to Heaven for using the bull in such a way as to cause such a vicious, scary death. Animals may not interpret fear the same as humans, but they do have the drive for life that the Creator gave them to survive and stay away from dangerous creatures. They do know to run, as the bull did or to fight. However animals do interpret a fearful situation, Maqoom had regret within him for causing such a feeling within the bull as well as causing it to lose its life. The bull may not have an eternal spirit, but Maqoom mentally, thoughtfully hoped that he would meet the bull again sometime on the other side and that the bull would recognize him as a friend. He smiled, almost having tears in his eyes, looked up to Heaven, smiling more broadly giving thanks to Heaven within his inner being for giving him a semblance of awareness of such a concept. It was actually, possibly meritorious of the bull, even though it did not have free will, to be utilized in saving future humans from losing their lives to the beast. Maqoom had full confidence, that if it was the Will of the Creator, he would see the bull again as friends. He spent the next hour and a half, digging up dirt to cover over the bull. He did not want to leave it openly exposed. One for respect towards Heaven as to not let it rot openly upon the earth, exposed to the sky and two, so that it was not a farm field for flies and their maggot offspring.

As Maqoom headed back to the barn, to turn in for the night in his hay bed, he walked past the barn, to the pasture gate. He used the last few minutes of light, to wedge back the pasture gate, tying it back as well for double protection from it closing and trapping an animal inside. The cows and horses already there could leave at their leisure as weather, thirst or predator drove them.

Chapter 8
Civilization

A t first light, Maqoom had both horses hitched to the wagon, ready to go. Maqoom rode his horse, with the four ladies sitting on the main wagon seat, it being large enough for them, plus some extra room. At each camp, the wagon would be placed downwind, at a distance to keep any creatures allured by its stink away from camp. He would look for clearings in the trees, where he could clear the ground of debris, get a fire going, then put the ladies by each other. After each would cover up with what blankets they had, he would then cover them all, with a cow hide canvas that the humanoid had in his barn, to help keep any rain or night dew off of them. Maqoom would then get a spot, just outside the ring of light emanating from the fire at its brilliance, where he could see the wagon and the ladies, just in case somebody would come upon the camp and try to cause trouble.

The first night out, Maqoom was thinking that after everything they had been through, he did not want to lose any of them to what he considered to be wild barbarians, who traverse the country sides looking for loot of any kind. That thought led him to think of his dad and Hans. He did not like the thought of associating his dad with wild barbarians, as he did not want to dishonor his dad. He verbally apologized to the Court of Heaven for the disrespect to his dad by the thought, disassociated his dad from it, falling to sleep within minutes.

Everyone slept well each night, with the exuberance of the ladies growing as they got closer to town. They were all overjoyed that they were free. They made the ride in five nights, arriving a couple miles outside of town on the sixth day, with thankfully, no incidents to speak of. By this time, the bodies were really stinking, so the wagon was parked, letting the wagon a couple miles out of town, in a large clearing to the side of the road. Two ladies each, took to each of the wagon team horses and on into town they went.

The size of the horses alone would have caused heads to turn with pause, but with two women on each, made heads turn with stare. Maqoom directed them to head straight to the sheriff's office, with him following. After hitching the horses to the post, which the two big horses could easily bust if they wanted, they went inside. The sheriff turned, looking at the crew of people who just invaded his office, "May I help you?"

Maqoom explained the situation to the sheriff and that the humanoid and the beast were just outside of town. He brought them to town, because he wanted to let local people know, who he figured knew about the humanoid, that it was dead and would not be bothering them anymore.

Sheriff Morris stated, "I want to gather a handful of men and ride out to see these creatures."

Maqoom asked, "Please give me just enough time to get the ladies settled, as I want to ride along too."

Sheriff Morris, granting his request stated, "Meet me back here, I'll have the other men ready."

Maqoom walked out with the ladies following. He headed to the hotel, asking, "How many rooms are available?

With the reply being, "Seven."

He said, "We will take five."

He instructed the clerk that the ladies were to each receive their own room and personal hot bath when they each were ready.

The clerk responded, "Supper and breakfast were at six and six with each going two hours, with lunch at noon; all to be paid extra at mealtime."

Each lady was given their key, and Maqoom his. He then asked the ladies to follow him, heading out the front entrance, straight to the general mercantile store. Walking in, Maqoom asked the attendant, "Do you have any ladies clothing to be had in this store?"

An affirmative "Yes, quite an extensive selection", was the forwarding reply from the clerk.

Following the attendant, they went back to a corner of the store, with a nice expansive display and variety of ladies clothing. Maqoom instructed the ladies to pick out what they want, keeping the attendant apprised of all the purchases and make your way back to the hotel for your hot bath. The four just stared at him, with one even having her mouth somewhat hanging open, like she did not comprehend what was happening, like it wasn't real or something.

Maqoom addressed the attendant asking, "How much do you think it will be for four women to dress themselves out, on average."

The attendant hesitated a couple seconds, then stated, "Per my experience, I cannot imagine them spending more than forty dollars."

Maqoom handed her sixty, stating, "When I come back, I'll get the change."

The clerk stated, "Sure, ok."

With that he headed to the livery, not even turning

around to look at the ladies. Once at the livery, he asked if there were any stalls available. Three, came the reply. Two of them were beside each other, so he brought the horses over, took their harnesses off, escorting each in their respective stall. The big horses could lift their heads up, but their ears would slightly touch the underside of the hay loft floor above. They seemed contented. He instructed food and water be given, paid the livery man then headed to the sheriff's office.

Chapter 9
The Burning

Inside the sheriff's office, were six other men, plus the sheriff. Maqoom walked in stating, "Ready!"

The ones sitting started to rise from their seats, so Maqoom spun around walking back out the door. One of the men asked about the two big horses, with Maqoom stating, "They belong to me and are not for sale."

The ride out was quiet, as none of the other men were actually sure what they were riding into or if there was anything to ride into. Once in the clearing though and first spotting the wagon, they all halted, with a number of horses nervous from the smell.

The sheriff said, "Let's ride around and come in from upwind, as where we are at this moment, it is not pleasant, and I do not want to get closer downwind."

They all came in from upwind, with Maqoom going in first to roll back the covering he had placed over the corpses. He held his breath doing his work, with him contemplating that the stench was actually causing his eyes to burn. Each of the others came in close then, jockeying to get in a good position to see inside the wagon. Even on their horses, they could not see fully in the wagon as it was so big and tall. They each saw plenty of what they needed to though.

The sheriff turned his horse around facing Maqoom. "You killed them?"

"Yes sir!"

"How?"

Maqoom related the story of each, not giving every minute detail but enough to draw a clear picture of what took place. Where the women were, how the humanoid came at him. How they buried the dead woman on the property where she died. How one of the ladies mentioning about men being directed around the corner of the house and not coming back. Using the bull as bait and eventually killing of the beast.

When he stopped, all the horses were turned around with the men looking and listening. One of the men spoke up stating, "I personally know six men who went out for that creature and did not come back."

A couple others each knew of one or two as well. Sheriff Morris stated, "Ok, you proved your point lad; now I want to burn this whole wagon with its load to ashes. Jeff and Will, you two as best as you can, get up there and get those guns and ammunition, handing them down to the others."

After the weapons and ammo were unloaded and at a safe distance, the sheriff instructed those who were with him to pack the entire underside of that wagon, from front to back with any burnable object they can gather. "Pack it in there!" were his instructions.

"Jim," he hollered, just before Jim got off his horse to follow the preceding instructions. "Ride back to town and get a gallon of kerosene from my office, bringing it back here."

Jim galloped off, with Maqoom thinking this is going to be one hot fire. Not long after Jim got back, the job was complete with the whole underside stuffed with logs, branches, bushes, dried grass, whatever the men could find that would burn. In the process, two rattle snakes were shot, being discovered as their natural built homes were being dismantled. A third one coiled and was going to strike but took a bullet to the head from another man standing by. Thankfully Maqoom thought, no one got bit. Tinder was sticking out from all four sides of that wagon. The sheriff poured the whole gallon inside the wagon, around the whole edge, holding his breath on the downwind sides, as the wind was blowing from the rear driver's corner to the front passenger's corner, across the wagon. The sheriff got the match between his chest and the wagon, striking it and letting it burn to full brilliance, per the little matches ability, reached out and pressed it close to the edge of the wagon, where he poured the last of the kerosene, which ran down the outside and inside simultaneously. It took a few seconds, but finally the kerosene lit, with the flame slowing walking its way into the wagon, around the entire perimeter of the inside. By the time the two flames met each other, it was already so hot they all had to get back about twenty feet, even there, feeling the heat fairly strong. Within ten minutes or so the whole pile was on fire, with the men now at least a hundred feet away and still able to feel the heat. The flames were well over fifteen feet in the air, with the height of the wagon helping to push the flames that high. After about thirty minutes the weight of the humanoid and the beast broke through what little remained of the wagon floor with the body fluids of both being boiled out of their bodies, turning to steam and rising up into the air. Eventually the fire got so hot, that what fluids did find their way out, instantly got evaporated from the heat, not even having the opportunity to turn to visible steam.

The men got up on the upwind side, on some rocks so they were all higher than the wagon, watching, smoking, chewing and having small talk amongst themselves. Maqoom hung out with them, listening to their stories of men who went after the beast but did not come back. On occasion one or two of them would look at Maqoom, wondering within themselves how this lad did this, when so many men before him could not.

As the fire started to lose its highest intensity, the sheriff stood up declaring, "We are out of here. I want you all to meet me in the sheriff's office in the morning, as we are going to come back and whatever is remaining shovel into that ditch, covering it with stones and earth." They all started to rise, with the sheriff adding, "Bring your shovels."

Chapter 10
Contentment

Maqoom was still standing with the sheriff back at town, as the others were dispersing out to their residences. Maqoom stated, "Goodnight sheriff" and turned to walk away.

"Son," the sheriff stated. Maqoom stopped and turned to face him. "We lived under the fear of that creature from well before I was ever on this earth. When I was a boy, when my father was a boy and even my Grandfather, who was one of the early founders of this town. We do not know if the humanoid, as you call it, was there for years before us or if he settled down after we got here, and after other towns started to crop up throughout the territory. But there has been enough fear and anger and torment, throughout the years, that a considerable bounty was placed on that creature's head, one thousand dollars. Tomorrow, after the burying, you and I will head to the bank, for you to collect what is yours."

Maqoom stepped closer to the sheriff so he did not have to speak any louder than necessary. "Sheriff, that is very meritorious of you, to come out and tell me that."

Immediately, the sheriff asked, "Are you accusing me of being a scoundrel?"

"No sir! It is a fact, that you did not know if I knew about the reward. Being so young and not local, you could definitely think that I did not know. There are plenty of people out there, badge or no badge who would work to secure that money for themselves. Because you did not do such a thing, being honorable to tell me, it is merit in your favor before the Court of Heaven. Verbalize it I do, as I want to witness before that Court that you are indeed deserving of said merit. It is an honor to me, a gift from Heaven to me, to be able to verbalize it and be a part of testifying on behalf of a fellow human, that you deserve merit for your decision, words and actions, that you thought, said and did what was right. No false accusation sheriff, but a verbalized testimony on your behalf."

Maqoom smiled, looking straight into the sheriff's eyes. Silence between them, then Maqoom smiled his pleasant smile with the sheriff reciprocating slightly. Maqoom took three steps, started to turn but then halted, stating "Sheriff!"

The sheriff half turned back around, "Yes Maqoom."

"Will you join me and possibly the ladies for supper at the boarding house? It will be about an hour before I am ready as I want to get a hot bath, so say six thirty?"

"Yes Maqoom, I will join you. Thank you!"

With that they both went their way. Maqoom was really joyful inside. The sheriff was honorable, with it indeed being so nice to be introduced to such fellow humans. He was heading for a hot bath and a room with a bed. Just before stepping off the road he stopped, looked up, still smiling, verbalizing a hearty "Thank You!" He asked the clerk for them to get his bath ready, then bounded up the stairs to ask the ladies if they would join him for supper. Knocking on the first door with no answer, he knocked on the second, again no answer and headed towards the third when the door to the fourth opened up, there they all were. He stood at the entrance, in the hall. One at the door, two on chairs and one on the corner of the bed.

"Come on in Maqoom!"

"No ma'am, I cannot. Hope you all have gotten the clothing you wanted and enjoyed your baths."

One of the ladies in the chair jumped up, blurting out, "You know, I have almost forgotten such nice things existed." They were all smiling and bubbly.

Maqoom smiled, as he was glad within himself, when people were pleased, joyful, contented. The one on the bed jumped up, stating "Oh! here is your change Maqoom. The total was thirty two dollars, so here is twenty eight."

"Thank you", said Maqoom.

"No, thank you!"

"Yes" stated all four, "thank you."

"Well, glad that you all seem to be pleased with the current state of things at this moment. Stopped by to ask if you would all join me for supper at six thirty, downstairs in the dining room."

"Yes, yes indeed", they all responded.

"Asked the sheriff to join us too, he seems like an honorable fellow. Do any of you mind?"

"No, certainly not", came the mutual response.

The youngest of the four piped up, "If you think he is honorable, then we trust him too."

Before walking away, Maqoom stated, "Sometimes I can be wrong about people, so make sure you all make your own decisions about a person, because Maqoom could be wrong, ok?"

"Ok" they all replied.

The sheriff was right on time, as was Maqoom and the ladies were too. The table selected was just inside the opening to the dining room, with one chair positioned just right, where that person could see the front door to the boarding house anteroom. Maqoom hesitated, so as to allow the sheriff to pick his seat, with the sheriff picking the spot that allowed the view. Maqoom thought good choice to himself, picking the seat to the right of the sheriff. At least here he was facing the opening to the dining room, being able to see out in the anteroom. The ladies all picked theirs, with exuberance shining on their faces.

Maqoom had heard that they served here, water for free, but that there was also a water they served for a nickel a glass, as it was hauled in from a spring over 20 miles away. Maqoom asked for the spring water for the table. They all ordered the chicken except for the sheriff, who got the steak. As the food was being placed on the table, Maqoom stated he wanted to say a blessing over the meal, doing so. Noticing there was a slice of bread with each plate, he stated, "Blessed are You our Heavenly Father, Who brings forth bread from the earth."

The meal was scrumptious. The ladies played a nice contest, to see who could pick out the spices used on the chicken, as it was the best any of them had ever eaten. Definitely some sage and rosemary, they determined and some black pepper too, but not sure of any others.

The sheriff stating that the steak was, "Just right, not tough, not chewy, not burnt but just right."

Maqoom was glad that all enjoyed the meal so much. Maqoom admitted as well, that "It was indeed delicious."

The chicken, with a nice baked potato, along with a nice slab of fresh butter melting on the inside of it, where the potato was sliced down the middle. Some green flakes on top too, with one of the ladies volunteering, "It was parsley." With the meal being sided with some green beans and sautéed, sliced mushrooms.

All were full. The water was just delicious with Maqoom noting that the glasses were empty long before anyone thought they would be, so he ordered another round. It was, "A meal of celebration and thanksgiving," he told his guests.

With the food gone, with hardly even a crumb showing on any plate, the waiter asked, "Would anyone like fresh apple pie?

"Oh," gushed one of the ladies, "Yes indeed! But I am so full, would any one share it with me?"

The other three stated they were full, and the sheriff demurred too. Knowing the lady wanted some, Maqoom smiled and said "Yes, I will share it with you, but only if you make sure to take half of the presented slice."

"Agreed!"

The piece of pie was served. with Maqoom allowing her to cut it. Right down the middle she did. As the plate came towards Maqoom, she was already taking a bite allowing an almost immediate sound of agreeableness come from her throat. "Oh, delicious she stated."

By now the other three were looking at Maqoom's slice, with him noticing. He slid it towards the far one, stating to "Please take a bite." Each of the three did, with only the heel of the crust being still on the plate as it got back to Maqoom. As the last one was still chewing, they realized what they did, all looking to Maqoom. He smiled, took his heel, eating it. "Ummm delicious he stated and gave them a big smile."

They all busted out laughing, how they almost gave him back an empty plate. It the midst of the laughter they apologized, with Maqoom joining in the laughter, stating "There was no harm done and that he was grateful they all enjoyed the meal so much and the pie too," which brought another round of laughter.

The sheriff even smiling as well.

Maqoom stated he wanted to give thanks for the food, with no one disagreeing with his desire. "Thank You Heavenly Father, for such bounty as You provide."

They all stated "Amen," as well as the sheriff too.

One asked him why he said the blessing and the thanks. Maqoom stated that, "the blessing was to acknowledge from Whom this bounty came from. The thanks is to say, 'Thank You,' for the fullness and contentment that a full meal brings to the human soul, as well giving thanks for nourishing the body too."

This led to another question from another of the group. "Maqoom!"

"Yes."

"You said the humanoid was on Noah's ark."

"Yes."

"You also gave some ideas earlier about how the tree creature survived the flood. Now that you've had more time to think of it, do you have any further ideas on how the tree creature did survive?"

"Well, that I am not so sure of. Maybe a humanoid had a couple in a plant pot, on a shelf in the ark." To which they all laughed at the thought.

"Maybe," one said "Or maybe a humanoid had some seeds in their pocket. Of course as stated earlier, maybe there were dormant seeds in the ground."

"Some things we just do not know the answer to," Maqoom brought forth. Adding; "However, my ignorance does not negate the Truth, so however it occurred, we know that it did."

Chapter 11
Anger

Crack, came the jolting sound of wood breaking under force from the front of the anteroom. Two men half running into the center of the anteroom, laughing and bumping into each other and swatting at each other with their hands. Both laughing and drunk. Instead of turning the door knob, they both hit the door with their shoulders, with such momentum it carried them into the center of the anteroom, with one hitting the floor on his side with a thump that sent a shock wave, which Maqoom could feel in his chair. A third man came in more slowly but laughing almost as hard as the first two.

The sheriff was up and heading to the anteroom. The ladies were all standing, facing the anteroom too. Maqoom was still seated, but rose slowly, stepping towards the opening, but against the opposite wall from their table. He could see the three men but was not out open within the dining room opening. The sheriff was at the men, helping the one to get up off the floor. "You men cannot just be busting other people's property," said the sheriff.

There was not time to even contemplate such would happen, but before the sheriff could even discourse another syllable, two guns were already punching into his belly. Both men pulled their guns, poking the sheriff in the belly, one on each side with the barrels pointing back towards his spine. The third man walked up with a smile on his face. He pulled the sheriff's gun from his holster telling the sheriff, "We do what we want! If you want to live sheriff, you stay out of our way."

The alcohol really had the man bolstered. Maqoom took two steps, clearing the side wall and being open in the anteroom. Without stopping, Maqoom said "You three, outside now!" As he walked past the man, Maqoom stated, loud enough for all to hear, "I do not want to paste the walls of this business with your brains, so out in the street big man."

Maqoom walked straight out the door, into the center of the street. No one else came out. Maqoom yelled, "Come on big man, let's go; all three of you, now!"

This would help empty the saloon, from where the men came from, putting pressure on them to act Maqoom's way. By the time the first of the three walked out, the saloon was already empty and watching with some taking bets. The first out was the one who appeared to be the leader, with one of his followers feet behind him. Both men walked to the center of the street, with a distance of about three feet between them. The third man came out with his gun still in the sheriff's belly. Maqoom yelled, "All three of you down here."

The leader yelled back, "NO! He stays with the sheriff."

Maqoom half looked at the man, still keeping the other two in clear eyesight. "After I kill these two, if I look up there and you still have your gun pointing at the sheriff, you will wish you were dead and in hell with these two, before I finish you off."

"Jim," came a shout from one of the guys at the saloon. The man who shouted came walking out of the crowd, towards the two men in the street. "What the hell are you doing Jim. You have to finish the job I am paying you for. Just get into the hotel and get some sleep. We have to leave early in the morning."

This fourth man was on Jim's left. Just as this man stopped to face Jim from his side, Jim turned grabbing him with both hands by his upper shirt. Jim jerked him, spinning him around so that the man was between himself and Maqoom. As Jim was swinging the man to clear his front, Jim already had his pistol in his right hand, coming up in front of his belly, somewhat covered between the two of them. Maqoom already had both guns out, with not one person seeing Maqoom draw, as they were all watching Jim and this fourth man. Maqoom's right gun cracked, with the bullet catching Jim in his left side, busting a rib going in, forcing its way right through the main center of his heart, giving Jim such a Jerk that his whole upper torso jerked making his head move back and forth in the opposite direction as his chest. The bullet broke a rib coming out the other side, with blood and lung spewing out onto the dust. It looked like a small, red dyed, tornado shaped rainstorm coming from a hole in Jim's right side. The second man with Jim, threw his hands in the air, and peed his pants, as the front of his pants almost instantly became darkened.

Maqoom walked straight towards him, both guns drawn. He noticed the man with the sheriff was already heading towards the men at the saloon entrance with the sheriff running after him, knocking him down at the entrance of an alley with the man stumbling down some steps, trying to keep his balance, but failing and hitting the ground hard. The sheriff was on him, having control of the man's gun, well before the man got his composure back. Maqoom walked straight up to the second man, hitting him hard in his ribs with both barrels, forcing the man to take a step back, trying to get away from the pain. With real anger, Maqoom sneered for the man to "Drop your gun belt or you are dead."

The man used both hands and was moving them fast, but Maqoom did not care, as he was watching that gun handle. If that gun even started to rise out of the holster, the projectiles from both of Maqoom's guns were going to be forcing their way through the man. The fourth man started walking back towards the saloon, shaken and wanting out of this mess. The sheriff was bringing his man over towards Maqoom and the man he was aiming his guns at. The belt and gun hit the dirt, with the sheriff picking them up. Before Maqoom could even put his guns away, people at the saloon were already asking each other if anyone saw him draw. Even the sheriff and the ladies did not see it. So, everyone was wondering, did they not pay attention or is Maqoom so fast, no one could follow it?

The sheriff took his two towards the jail, with Maqoom looking up at the ladies on the hotel boardwalk. They looked extremely harried, so Maqoom instantly, almost without thought, smiled at them, trying to reassure them and calm them. He kept his conscious thought on the fourth man as he walked towards the saloon, as well at the other men at the saloon entrance. If any man made a move with a gun, he was going to drop them.

Maqoom walked up onto the boardwalk where the ladies stood, smiled at them stating, "You all have been through much worse." One of them shot back, "Like drawing a gun and shooting, we were worried about you, not us. The anger was so real that which we saw in you and then you smile at us, like nothing happened."

Maqoom hesitated a moment. "Anger is a tool he told them. You pick up a hammer to build a house. When you are done for the day, you lay it down. So too anger. You pick it up to achieve a goal and when done with it, you put it down."

The ladies were fine thankfully, and the men were making their way back into the saloon. Maqoom turned to check on the sheriff, but the street was empty. He started to take a step towards the jail, when the door opened with the man on the street coming out, with the sheriff behind him. Sheriff Morris got a bucket of water, directing the man to walk around the corner of the jail away from the saloon. When the man stepped back out, he was totally soaked on his front. The sheriff had doused him, trying to wash out the urine. They both went back into the jail, with the sheriff reappearing shortly, laying out the man's pants over the hitching post, to dry. Maqoom thought to himself, how respectful Sheriff Morris is, that he did not soak the man out on the street, in full view of onlookers; very kind and thoughtful. He did not want to humiliate the man any more than the man already had done to himself.

Maqoom smiled, and stated verbally, with hardly more than a whisper, as he was addressing the Heavenly Court that, "It was very meritorious of the sheriff to be so respectful to a fellow human. Especially one, whom moments before was lined up to kill another." The whisper before the Court, was to be a witness, to testify on behalf of Sheriff Morris and his act of respect for a fellow human.

Maqoom headed towards the boarding house entrance, as he wanted to pay the bill. The meal had come to an end, so he saw no reason to go back to the table. After paying for the meal, he turned to go to the jail, but all four ladies were in the anteroom. He walked up to them asking, "Would you like to share a bottle of wine or have some water? I am going to go visit the sheriff, but if any or all of you would like to sit at a table in the dining room, it is my desire that you be comfortable and enjoy yourselves."

One responded "Wine please," with a second saying "Yes, wine please", with both turning to face one another, nodding their heads up and down in agreement and approval, smiling as if it was a holiday treat.

The two others, simultaneously stated, "Just water."

One of the latter two made her eyes open up wide with excitement, stretched her neck slightly towards Maqoom, asking, "The spring water that we had with the meal?", with a smile slowly spreading across her face.

Maqoom looked over at the attendant, "Two wines and two waters, the spring water, to be served to the ladies at whatever table they pick." He paid for the drinks, stating "If they want more, please give it to them, as I will pay when coming back through."

"Yes sir!" was the reply.

The ladies as a group said, "Thank you."

Maqoom acknowledged, stating "You are welcome."

With that he headed towards the entrance. As he walked out onto the boardwalk, he saw the fourth man had come back to the body, standing over it. Maqoom, walked straight toward him, stopping just an arm's length away. The man looked up at him, not speaking. Maqoom spoke stating, "If this man has any money on him, it should go towards fixing the boarding house door jam."

"Ok," spoke the man.

The man then checked his pockets and boots. Coming up with some money, the man stated "Let's go talk to the owner."

Maqoom turned sideways, gesturing for the man to go first. The man complied. There was enough money to pay for the jam, with some remaining. This fourth man suggested, "With the remainder, it should for the burial."

Maqoom stated, "Lets walk to the sheriff's office."

Sheriff Morris informed the man how much it would be, stating "This is appropriate to do, so the city does not have to pay for it. Thank you for thinking of it."

After paying the sheriff the amount stated, there were still a couple dollars remaining. Sheriff Morris motioned to the saloon with his head, stating "You might as well go have a drink on Jim."

The man nodded his head slightly a couple times, looking at the money. Looking up at the sheriff, then at Maqoom, he nodded his head again, then turned to walk away.

Sheriff Morris broke the silence, "If you want your men, pick them up early in the morning."

The man did not turn around, but stated clearly, "Ok sheriff" and kept walking.

Sheriff Morris went and got two beers from the saloon, bringing them back to the jail. The sheriff and Maqoom sat out on the boardwalk in front of the jail, drinking their beers and talking. Maqoom told Sheriff Morris, "Very disappointed I am in myself, in that I was exceedingly angry when the episode was occurring, that it was not just show, but I felt it within me."

Sheriff Morris came back with, "You did very well. You showed your anger to get their attention, then you let it drop like a tool. As a matter of fact, if you want a job, I need a deputy."

However, Maqoom knew within himself, that he had to be more alert for that emotion getting a hold of him, as it could lead to some really bad consequences. For himself and others.

It was past ten when they finally, parted company.

Maqoom liked sheriff Morris very much, being very tempted when the sheriff offered him a deputy job, as the town was growing, with one sheriff not quite being enough anymore. Maqoom demurred, as he had "At least one more town to go to."

Sheriff Morris called out to Maqoom, "Tell the ladies that after we get back in the morning, we will start work on getting them all to where they want to go."

Maqoom had turned, half facing the sheriff and looking at him. "Ok," stated Maqoom and raised his right arm and hand to wave goodnight.

The sheriff waved back, with Maqoom turning and heading in for the night. The ladies were already out of the dining room and onto their rooms, so he would have to give them the sheriff's message tomorrow. Maqoom opened the window of his room slightly, so that any street noise might hopefully wake him, as he was concerned the soft bed might make him sleep too long. *Wow*, Maqoom thought, that mattress is soft, then he was out.

Chapter 12
The Burial

Wₕen Maqoom stepped out onto the boardwalk, most of the men were already at the jail. The trail boss handler was stepping out of the jail, with the two other men behind him. The sheriff had given them their guns, just before getting on their horses. The three rode out of town, in the opposite direction that the sheriff and his crew were heading this morning. Maqoom was on his horse at the jail, as the last of the remaining men arrived. "Let's move out", Sheriff Morris pronounced.

There was still smoke rising from the ash heap. More physical matter remained, than what Maqoom thought would be there, considering the heat of the flames. Some men started to dig a trench, as others gathered rocks to be used to put over what gets buried. They were not going deep, maybe three foot. If one got downwind, the smell was somewhat strong, with the burning flesh of the humanoid. There were some big bones still remaining of him. The tree creature was completely consumed. Maqoom, could not tell any part of him was remaining. After the rocks were collected, the trench was moving along nicely, so some commenced to shovel in the remains of the burning, into the ditch. The area was cleaned up, the remains covered in dirt, with the rocks piled on top about a foot deep, with the men heading back before ten.

Riding into town, clearing the corner onto the main street, the first thing they noticed, were the ladies waiting at Sheriff Morris's office. Maqoom did manage to get the message from the sheriff to one of them that he saw in the anteroom before heading out that morning, asking her to tell the others. At the sheriff's office, the sheriff thanked the men as well as Maqoom for their help. Some of the men, thanked Maqoom for getting rid of the menace, they were glad to help. The sheriff had a private meeting with the four ladies, in his office while Maqoom stayed out. Maqoom did not want to influence them in any way, as he already knew he would be heading out soon.

The sheriff knew of the town close to one of the ladies, with it being only a two day stage coach ride away. She was on the coach that afternoon, as the coach pulled in just in time for lunch, watered the horses and headed out. Maqoom paid for the coach and handed the girl, out of view of the others, one hundred dollars. She could not believe it and was astonished at such a sum all in one place, especially in her hands. He had it in smaller denominations, so she would not have to flash large bills around for others to see. She thanked him profusely with Maqoom stating "Your welcome."

One heading home. He was thankful and smiling as she rode away, that he could be of help in another person's life like that, to help get her home.

One did not want to go back to any home that she came from. Maqoom asked her, "Well what is it you require for your plans?" then he bought it for her.

A healthy horse, of her choosing. Nice saddle and bags and a 45 revolver with belt and ammunition, along with a repeating rifle. Maqoom wanted to see her handle the weapons, so all of them took the sheriff's wagon outside of town for a shoot. She did really well using both, with the sheriff and Maqoom both realizing she knows what she is doing, with both agreeing neither of them want to be who she is sighted on. The next morning after a good night's rest and full belly in the morning, the group saw her off, with Maqoom doing the same for her, as the first by giving her a hundred dollars in small bills. She looked him straight in the eyes stating, "Thank you Maqoom", with liquid forming around the peripheral of her eyes, but not quite enough to cause a stream down her cheeks.

He smiled, stating "You take care of yourself."

She nodded, got on her horse like a seasoned cow hand, prodded it in the sides and off she went, heading north east out of town.

The sheriff could not figure out where the other two came from and they were not helping much with any landmarks they were describing. Both the General Store and the boarding house needed help, so they asked the sheriff if they could stay in town. He saw no reason that they could not, it being a free society and all, "Glad to have you", he stated.

Instead of them having to pay rent, until they got on their feet, Maqoom bought them a two room house, just down from the sheriff and within easy walking distance to both the store and the inn. Really it was the sheriff's house, which he hardly ever slept in since the death of his wife, he preferring to stay at the jail. The jail was his home for now. Maqoom drew it up though, so as to put it in both ladies' names. He also gave each of them one hundred dollars, of which they were completely overwhelmed. The house alone was such a blessing, then to get what some men do not see in a whole year, all in one day was almost too much for each of them. Maqoom suggested they each open a bank account and put some away, always trying to add to it. They agreed, with the sheriff making the introductions to the bank president.

Everything happened so fast with the ladies, that Maqoom still had not visited the bank man to give him the money. Asking the sheriff to go with him, they entered the man's private office, this being one of the bigger banks Maqoom had been in, each being offered a chair, which they took.

After introductions by the sheriff, Maqoom commenced to speak, "The main reason I was heading to this town, was because it had become known to me that a considerable sum of money was stolen some years back by two men."

"Three, the sheriff" remarked.

"One of them is buried out in the town cemetery, the bank man retorted. "Yes Maqoom, five thousand, one hundred dollars they got away with. It really hurt a lot of people. Why do you inquire of this Maqoom?"

Maqoom had his saddle bag over his knees, pulling out of one side wads of money. He counted out five thousand, one hundred dollars, laying it on the man's desk in nice neat stacks. The man was struck dumb just about, with the sheriff staring between the money and Maqoom. The desire of them both, to know what this was about, was so thick in the air, they did not have to ask outright. Maqoom told them, "One of the men was my father, who has been killed. After which, my mother and I found this money. My mother went back East, while I myself commenced traveling from bank to bank giving back what was stolen."

They just could not believe it. They just could not believe it. Repeating three or four times between the two of them, that they just could not believe this was happening. Maqoom smiled, stating "It is my hope that all the families who lost money are still in the area, so they can get their money back."

The sheriff stated, "All but one of the families remain. Most of the men who rode with us to handle the menace are some of them."

The bank man said, "I have to get the books out and start to work to see who gets what. Thank you Maqoom, very much, for what you have done. Also, there is a $250.00 reward for this money. That is yours now." The banker counted out money he had retrieved from the safe, the stated amount.

Sheriff Morris stood up stating, "There is also a reward for the creature. We have been increasing it for years, trying to get someone, hoping someone would be able to collect someday."

"That is right", the banker stated. "Sheriff I am glad you mentioned that. Was almost to the point of thinking no one would ever collect it, just about forgetting it is here." He walked back over to the safe for this money. Pulled out a case, opening it for Maqoom. "Nine hundred and seventy five dollars are in here Maqoom. This is yours too."

Sheriff Morris told the banker what Maqoom did for the ladies and how he helped them.

Maqoom stating, "It was a blessing from Heaven to be able to help them and be useful." Maqoom sensed the sheriff was wondering about the money he gave the ladies, so he stated "None of the money given to the ladies came from what was found, of my Fathers bundle. That was money from the sale of the farm that Mother split with me and also rewarded money from other banks."

As they were leaving, Maqoom asked the banker about the next town and if they had a robbery.

The banker stood up, "Yes Maqoom they did have a robbery, about a year before us. They basically now have a tyrant of a sheriff, who will kill on a whim. Man or woman, child too. Almost want to ask you not to go there, as you may not come out of that place. After the robbery, a man by the name of Charlie Brandt took the sheriff's job, becoming a complete tyrant over the years. He runs that area over there like it is his own country, with no one but him in charge. From what I recall, it was about two thousand dollars."

Maqoom stated, "Well I have 2100 remaining, so that sounds like my next stop." Maqoom thanked the banker.

The banker replied, "Thank you Maqoom!"

As the sheriff and Maqoom sat out in front of the jail, after a nice lunch with beers in their hands, the sheriff added onto the bankers warning about Charlie Brandt. "He has turned cold Maqoom. Two times now his men have been here tracking someone. When I tell them I have not seen the person, they do not take it well, commencing to tell me what I am going to do and how I am going to help. The second time, I pulled my gun, telling them to never come back to this town, as they do not own this town. Thankfully, the men that helped us are a close knit group and backed me up both times. They know if they come here, they will have to fight more than just me. Have not seen them in over a year."

"Maqoom, one of the men they were after, I hid. Did not want to turn him over to them, not letting them know I had him. The man told me that no one is allowed to leave the area. No one can buy or sell to another without permission and that Charlie believes he owns everything and everyone. People may be passing through and if Charlie likes what they have, he will kill some, forcing the remaining to stay as his subjects basically, like he is a king. Maqoom, if you ride in that town, Charlie could kill you at any time for any reason or for no reason, if that is what he wants to do. Agree with Ben, you should not go there. Give the money to charity, letting it be."

Maqoom stated that, "Charlie sounds no different than the humanoid, except Charlie seems more human, beating his soul down into surrender, like stuffing to many clothes in a carry case and pressing hard to get the other half to close. Probably he has pushed his soul so far down, that there is no more communication with his spiritual side. Some people can get that way sheriff. The soul just finally gives up, even leaving the body sometimes, with the person ending up like a humanoid, but with much more intelligence as far as interpersonal relationships and manipulating people to get what they want."

"Or killing them," the sheriff added, "To get what they want."

Maqoom knew he was going, with the sheriff acquiescing to the fact, getting up to go buy them another beer.

Chapter 13
The Calm Before the Storm

It was a blue bird sky day, when Maqoom rode into Charlie Brandt's town. As he was riding the trail through the woods earlier that morning, the birds singing vocals was an euphony of sounds, so pleasing to his spirit that he thought his smile was from ear to ear. The fruit trees along the edge of the road, were blooming mixing in the aromatic incense of sweet smells, with the symphony of sound around him, his internal being wanting so much to give praise, that he looked up at that sky, smiling with such gratefulness inside his soul, pouring out without word to The Creator, like an offering on the Alter of antiquity, when the Temple still fully stood. He thought of his mother, giving thanks for allowing him to have the mother that he was chosen for. Personally, he sensed that he was not worthy of such a mother, but he immediately dismissed it, gratefully, thankful within, for being allowed to have Sarah as his mother. In an effort, to provide some kind of beneficial testimony on behalf of his father, he made mental note that the father, mother combination that he had, made him who he is and if there was or is ever any good that comes from Maqoom being alive, he wanted the credit to be attributed to his mother and father, for their contribution. Even the ability to give thanks to God, to obey a command of God, how man is to live with man, is something, if he would succeed in doing these, could be considered as meritoriousness on behalf of his mother and father. He did not hate his father, he wanted to help him, on the other side, where he now was. So, the reason for him trying to find anything good that he could think or say, that would be beneficial testimony on his father's behalf. Also, he prayed for that meritoriousness, righteousness combination to be carried forward and attributed to any future children, grandchildren, to all generations, that may be through his mother. It is a God given blessing to be used to find goodness, righteousness in fellow humans and to bring it to the attention of the Heavenly Court. To testify so to speak on behalf of those who have come before, those who are and those who are to be, through those who are or have come before and even through those who are to be. The continuum of the timeline, from generation to generation, ties all humans together. That oneness of existence is why a peasant in an impoverished country can, through words, actions, deeds, thoughts or the proper lack thereof of any or all, can affect multitudes of humans throughout the earth, of which they are never going to meet in this lifetime, nor are the ones he is affecting so positively going to know it was him until the World to Come. Maqoom was filled with such joy, such ecstasy to be thinking that he was useful to his fellow humans, as the Creator guided him, directed him, making him aware of situations where he can say or think such testimony for his fellow humans, regardless of the timeline, they were, are or may be in.

He burst out a "Hallelujah" right there, looking up to the sky as he said it, letting it linger as long as there was enough air coming out of his lungs to make it seem like the vocal cords were still producing the sound of the last syllable.

His smile got so big, he thought the corners of his lips

may crack as he thought that maybe the angels in Heaven would pick up where he left off, turning his singular shout of praise into a crescendo of Heavenly upheaval. "Hallelujah" he yelled again out into space, again holding the last note until there was no real air crossing his vocal cords, but his mind had picked up the note carrying it forward. The ecstasy was so strong within him, that again he forced himself to stop, thinking his soul would burst right forth, dropping his body to the ground dead, of which he was not to pick the time of death, the Creator would.

Maqoom was not in a hurry to die, but the thought was real, the possibility present. He rode along, content with the world. As he was noting his surroundings, he mentally realized there was a clearing up ahead, maybe two to three hundred yards away. He was back in this world now, settling himself within, to be coherent about what was transpiring about him.

Chapter 14
Introductions

A s he came out of the woods, the town was about 500 yards before him. It was clear cut all around like that. It sat in the center of a large, manmade clearing. No one could approach from any direction without being noticed. Not sitting on a horse anyway.

Maqoom rode into town, riding straight to the bank hitching post. He only saw two or three other people, but only briefly as they seemed to all step inside as he rode into view, still some distance from town. He was uncertain within himself, why he was not sure if it was two or three. Did he see them or not? He let the thought go, focusing on the task at hand. The only person visible as he hitched his horse was a deputy sitting in a chair on the boardwalk, outside the bank. Maqoom went around the back of his horse from the left side, lifting his saddle bags from the horse and onto his shoulder.

As he stepped up onto the boardwalk, the deputy stood, telling Maqoom, "Stop, where are you going?"

"Inside the bank," Maqoom replied.

"No you are not," the man said. "No one is allowed in the bank without approval and you are not approved, or I would have been told."

Maqoom stated, "Well, I have some business with the banker, of which I would like to talk with him."

"About what?" stated the man.

"About giving him some money," stated Maqoom.

The man lowered his chin some, turned his head slightly, squinted his eyes and stared at Maqoom, like he was trying to read his mind or something. Maqoom waited. Finally, the man walked to the door and knocked. A man opened the door, was told this stranger wants to give you some money, the man then stepped onto the boardwalk.

Maqoom asked the banker, "Has your bank been robbed some years before and if so, how much was taken?"

"$2100.00," came the reply.

Maqoom said, "Good, for that is exactly what I have remaining."

Maqoom slowly took the saddle bags off his shoulder, opened up the left side, allowing the man to peer in. The man reached in, grabbed a couple packs, dropped them back in the saddle bag stating, "I'll be right back."

He was back in a minute with a bag of his own. As he would take money out of Maqoom's bag, the man would count it, then drop it in his own bag. Three men walked across the street from the livery stable, standing about ten feet or so behind Maqoom's horse. Being fully aware of them, he tried to keep track of them, without letting on too much that he did not trust them and was intentionally watching them, though not directly. So it was three he thought, making a mental note that he has to be more observant.

"Twenty one hundred on the nose," the man stated. He looked up from his counting, staring at Maqoom.

Maqoom stated, "The men who took it are dead, so I traveled here so it could be given back to those whom it was taken from."

The banker did not thank him, just turned around, walked into the bank and closed the door. For Maqoom, he just wanted to leave, now.

Turning, he stepped off the boardwalk onto the dirt street that ran through town, put his saddle bag across his horse and stepped back, so he could see all three men on his left, with the man on the boardwalk on his right. The middleman on his left stated, "We want to see in your saddle pack."

"That is personal property and there is no reason for you to have to look in it, so no."

Just as Maqoom was wondering what this was all about, a rifle cracked. The bullet went into the side of his horse, making his horse arch its back like a cat stretching after a nice sleep. As the bullet cleared the horse's body on the side Maqoom was standing by, hot blood and meat peppered all over the right side of Maqoom's upper body and face, making him blink just slightly and turn his head ever so slightly away from the exit wound. Before the horse's belly hit the ground, Maqoom had both guns drawn, with the middleman on his left and the bank guard on the boardwalk both hit at the same time. Chest shots, through their sternums and out their backs. Bones shattering with blood and lung blowing out the exit holes. Before they hit the ground, Maqoom was already squeezing a shot on the far left man. The man was just raising his handgun, when Maqoom's bullet hit his chest, nicking his spine, slightly spinning the man to his left. Maqoom noticed the gun drop straight down into the holster from which it was coming from, as the man's grip relaxed from the pistol butt. Maqoom swung on the third man on his left, the far right one, who did have his pistol cleared of its holster. Maqoom was so calm and aware. It was like everything was in slow motion, with him knowing every move of all the players and fully aware that he had plenty of time to do what he had to do. Just before Maqoom squeezed his trigger, the other man pulled his trigger, firing lead. Maqoom could clearly see that the barrel was pointed down too far and to his left, thereby the bullet hit the ground three feet in front and two feet to the left of Maqoom. The bullet ricocheted off the ground, hitting a post on the boardwalk with a thud as it sunk into the wood, ripping as it went clear through, throwing splinters of wood on the side of the building wall behind it, with the bullet entering the building. The man shot out of fear and he knew it. For as Maqoom was squeezing his trigger, the man's eyes looked directly into Maqoom's showing the terror of the knowledge that he was dead, though he was still alive at the moment. The bullet tore through the man, with the man throwing his hands out in front of himself, as if he could stop the bullet. The bullet went through the palm of one hand, tore off the forefinger of the other, before ever hitting his chest, blowing blood and foam out his back. He hit the ground hard, as his legs immediately gave way under him, since no more sensory input from the brain could cross the divide which opened up within his spine, as the bullet completely severed it hitting into the building wall across the street with a thud. The crack of the guns were echoing off the walls of the buildings making them sound sharper to the ear than otherwise would be the case. It was a frightful sound, like a jab of lightening, too close for comfort.

Without delaying, Maqoom was turning away, turning towards the alley beside the bank, when the rifle cracked again. This time, the bullet went through the space that contained Maqoom's head just an instant before. He heard the bullet cracking through the air, ripping space apart as it went, it was so close to him. He was so aware and so calm he noticed. Running towards the alley, he was off the street and just out of sight when the rifle cracked again, splintering the corner of the bank wall. The man is panicked Maqoom thought and he wants it over. He does not want Maqoom hunting him. Maqoom ran, down the alley full bore, at the end as he turned left, he was not concerned that the man may be over there too. Maqoom was so aware of so much. Sounds, sight, sky, tree line, ground, buildings, everything seemed to be known to him at this moment, yet he was running full force, but it all seemed to be standing still for him. Like he had all the time in the world to acknowledge the existence of everything around him and what it was all doing. He had this sense of oneness before, as he came down the steps at the boarding house to fight the cowboys in the street. But, before he could really become aware of it and what it meant, he got so angry at them, that it left him. His anger pushed it out, made it go back to where it came from. No anger this time though. He was calm, doing what has be done to stay alive and kill those who have made themselves his enemies.

He ran past the buildings, turning left around the building where the man had stationed himself, shooting while supporting his rifle with elbows on the boardwalk. If the man was still there, Maqoom was just going to shoot him. There was no slowing, no concern about taking a bullet. As he cleared the next turn, back out into the main street, the man was maybe 50 yards in front of him, knees half bent, body slightly arched over as the man was trying to take his time, keeping a low profile and looking between each building and down every alley. Maqoom cleared the distance to less than 30 yards, when the man finally realized something was coming, half turning to look behind himself. The man spun around, bringing the rifle up so he could aim. Maqoom brought both pistols up, clanging their barrels together in midair. Just as his barrels hit each other, he pulled both triggers, just under 20 yards away. Both bullets hit the man's sternum, ripping easily through the flesh and blood internals, then hitting the spine together, completely shattering it making the man's shoulders jerk forward as if his hips were just below his armpits. As the shoulders jerked forward, his head jerked backwards. The skin, tendons and muscles prevented the shoulders from folding down too far, but stretched they were, thereby causing the shoulders to jerk back the other way towards his rear and the head to swing forward in the opposing direction. His shoulders and head did this opposing dance, as his body was pushed to the ground, hitting it with far more force than just from its weight alone. As he hit, the dust of the street came up around his sides, settling on his shirt and face to give him a slight dusty look all over his upper body. The blood coming out of the man's chest, at first red, then turning darker as the dust was settling upon it. At first the man's chest was light brown, like dust settling on a solid object, but then the dust absorbed the blood into itself, turning the chest to a dark maroon.

Maqoom jumped up onto the boardwalk, putting his back to the building, away from the window, then squatted down to watch. His breathing was not harder than if he had just taken a run for the fun of it. He was calm, fully aware, with it being such an experience, that he did not want to lose it. As he realized there was no one else trying to kill him at this moment, it did leave him gradually. By the time he stood up, he was the normal Maqoom, though normal would not ever be what he was before. This is a new normal, but still not what he was just moments before. Taking the empty cases out of the revolvers, putting fresh rounds in, he holstered both. Still he hesitated for a couple more minutes, looking and listening, striving to sense anything wrong before he would step out into the street.

After those minutes, he walked down the boardwalk to his horse, got his saddle and saddle bag off and from under it, carrying them across the street to the livery stable. "Mind if I keep these in here for a spell," Maqoom asked the man, who stood in the entrance to the livery through the whole ordeal that just took place.

"No that is fine," came the reply. "It is going to belong to me fairly soon anyway, so you might as well carry it in, saving me from having to do it."

Maqoom dropped the saddle and bags in an empty stall, turned, looking at the man thinking he was going to draw on him any second in order to fulfill the words that just spilled forth from his mouth. "What do you mean belong to you?"

"Two riders headed out of town, heading southwest, before you killed the last one. They are heading to the sheriff's house to get help. It is about an hour round trip ride, so I would say in about an hour, your belongings will be mine, as you will be dead."

"Does anyone around here bury people?"

"I do," said the livery man.

"How much for the five and the horse?"

"One dollar for each and five dollars for the horse."

Maqoom did not quibble. Maqoom handed him a ten. "May I take some of the water in the trough?"

"Yes, no charge."

Maqoom picked up an empty bucket, filled it with water, then took a step away from the trough, getting down on his knees. He took a couple healthy gulps of water, using the remainder of the water to wash off the blood and horse meat from his face, making sure to turn away from the bucket so as to not splash blood or meat in the bucket. Grabbing his rifle, heading to the southwest corner of town. He went to the woods edge, sat down by a tree trunk in the shade and waited.

Wasn't long before he heard the hoof beats coming closer. He stood, walked to the center of the road and waited. The men, five of them, came around the bend about 80 yards away, at a full gallop, but slowed to a walk as they noticed Maqoom standing in the middle of the road. The five of them walked their horses straight to Maqoom, stopping about ten feet away.

"What are you doing here son?" the man who appeared to be the leader stated.

"Two men rode out of town of which I presume, they went to get reinforcements. Figured I would rather fight you out here as compared to in town."

"You are kind of an arrogant bastard, for you did not even know how many of us would be coming. You believe you can whip an army?"

"Do the best I can and with the help of Heaven, nothing is impossible."

The man stared briefly at Maqoom, spurred his horse, walking him out and around Maqoom's right side. The others followed suite, single file one at a time. Maqoom stood his ground, twisting enough to be able to see those who past him as well as those still yet to pass. After they all had passed him, Maqoom smiled to himself thinking that is a wise man right there, someone who Maqoom, if he has to deal with anymore, he had better keep track of. Walking back to town, he walked close to the building at that end of town, then out onto the boardwalk. Two men were sitting on their horses in front of the bank, one man was on the boardwalk standing by the bank guard, with the boss man and another not visible, though their horses were next to the other two. Maqoom walked to the livery, took a chair putting it in the shade of the entrance, sat and watched. When the two men came out of the bank, Maqoom stood up and started walking straight towards all of them. Stopping about twenty yards away, he watched. The boss man looked at him for a few seconds, then walked to his horse, mounted, as did the other two on the ground, with all five riding out of town to the southeast.

Chapter 15
Evil for Evils Sake

Maqoom walked back to the livery, took his same chair, sat down and looked up. He contemplated what just happened, the direction this may go next, why did the man not draw and where was he going? The livery man took a chair dropping it beside Maqoom. Maqoom did not have to ask questions, as this man liked to talk.

"That was Ben Hensen, the leader of those five. He is Charlie Brandt's second. Charlie is the sheriff. After the bank robbery years back, Charlie killed the sheriff in a confrontation, as Charlie was blaming him for not protecting the town's money. Charlie took the badge and has not taken it off since. The position has gone to his head, changing him from what appeared to be a normal man into a monster currently."

"Why a monster?" Maqoom asked.

"Never knew Charlie to kill anyone before the sheriff, but after that it is like he discovered he likes it. The killings kept getting crueler and crueler, to the point where I could not ride with him and almost lost my life for it. To this day, I am uncomfortable anytime Charlie is in town, as no one knows what may trigger him to kill.

"Some years ago a man stole from him, some personal items out of his house. Charlie got his men, of which I was one of them, trailing the man until we finally got him about four days out. He had us hang the man from a firm tree limb, shooting almost straight out from its trunk, as it was trying to get to the sun, past the limbs over it. We hung the man by his wrists, with his feet about six inches from the ground. Charlie then walked up to him, gave him a sermon on not stealing, then slit his belly from below his belly button to his center chest bone. Then Charlie made two horizontal gashes, one on each side of the vertical gash, a couple inches below the belly button about four inches each way. The man's innards washed out of his belly, landing on the ground and at his feet, as well as on his feet. Oh, what a howl, as the man kicked, squirmed and howled like a wounded beast. The louder the howling the bigger Charlie's grin became. Charlie had to jump back some to not get splattered with the man's bowels, as well as not get kicked by his squirming. Charlie's face was alight. His smile was from ear to ear, his eyes were wide with his body almost shaking from giddiness, as sounds like a baby cooing were coming from his vocal cords. Right then and there I thought to myself that Charlie was going to be addicted to this, like some men crave alcohol, so would Charlie crave this barbarianism.

"We then lit a nice fire, some fifty yards off, with Charlie taking a seat on a log he had some men carry over for him. He then rolled cigarettes and drank coffee, just watching the man hang there, moaning. I wanted to shoot the man, just to stop the moaning, but I did not dare mention anything other than what Charlie wanted to do. After dark, they had to keep the fire going, just enough to allow us to see the man, but not so big as to completely scare off any scavengers in the area. Eventually, some raccoons came by, cautiously sniffing at the man, taking daring darts in toward the innards, nipping at them with their mouths, or clawing at them with their paws. The man would try to kick at them, but his feet were tied at the ankles, so all he could do was try to jerk his body, in order to make his feet swing, in an attempt to scare the animals. This made his wrists hurt from the scraping of the ropes, as well as the open slits down and across his belly and howl, oh he would howl. Sometimes I wake up from dreams hearing that howl. Finally though, the animals got brave, moving in to grab innards, pulling and clawing to get their share. Grabbing innards in their mouths, then running off like they do to keep from sharing it, only to have it come taut thereby pulling the man ever so slightly and spinning the animal around, as it was not going to let go of its prize. Oh, that man would howl each time, screaming and yelling, jerking his body; it makes me shudder just talking about it now. By then, some opossums showed as well, with them joining the feast. They were eating his innards, as he was still alive and watching. With him jerking so much, the innards got tangled about his feet, so on occasion, when an animal would bite into the man's innards, the animal's teeth would bite into his feet as well, which would set him off again with that howl. The animal not knowing he had more than just innards in his mouth, would snarl and growl, shaking its head, pulling back trying to get its catch off somewhere to itself. The man would be jerking trying to get the animal off his foot. At one point jerking so hard, that he brought the biggest raccoon of the bunch, completely off all four feet and into the air, with the animal never letting go, even pulling harder when its feet got back on the ground, growling, snarling and pulling all the while, with the man yelling at the top of his lungs, squirming all about trying to get free of the animal. Oh, I thought I was going to burst out yelling and had to turn away, hoping that Charlie would not notice. I was terrified of Charlie at that point, thinking he could do this to me. There were times when I could hear my heart beating in my ears, pounding and I thought I might die right there, with so many chemicals surging through my body, that I was shaking as if I was an alcoholic looking for my first drink of the day. Don't see how the man lasted so long and maybe it was not as long as it seemed, but it seemed like it would never stop.

"Charlie was on the edge of the log, with a smile so big, it made me disgusted with him. I looked away so he would not notice that I disapproved by reading my face. Then I got behind him some, so hopefully he would not catch a glimpse of me. Did not want to look, but I kept finding myself looking, staring as I never saw such a thing and it pulled my attention to it, like flowers pull in bees. My mind was racing, telling me not to look, but at the same time the desire to look, to watch was overpowering, as I did watch. At one point a raccoon got inquisitive, jumping up on the man's leg, sinking those claws on his front and back feet deep into the man, just like he would if he were climbing a tree. That raccoon climbed, as the man was jerking and screaming at the top of his lungs, trying to get that raccoon off of him or get help to do so. The man was sobbing, yelling, jerking all around as best he could, with the blood from his wrists that were rubbed raw from the ropes, running down his arms and his sides. That raccoon climbed, losing footing here or there as the man jerked, only to sink its claws back into the man. It was up to his waist, when the man's jerking caused it to lose its grip, that it started to fall towards the ground. Thought for sure that the man had managed to get the animal off of him, but the raccoon caught itself by its claws in the man's meat, ripping and tearing, as flesh is not like tree bark, at which point the man howled out so loud I did look away; then it got quiet.

"Do not know if the man actually died right then or later, but it was not much longer after that point, that the man went quiet and still. Charlie got up and laid himself down for the night, with the rest of us following suite."

"Another time, on a cattle branding outing, a man had made fun of Charlie, mocking his walk and cocky attitude. Right in front of Charlie he did it. A little too much whiskey with supper made him free I guess, but he lost his life for it, the hard way. Charlie had him taken and hung by his ankles. This time, the man's head was just inches from the ground. Charlie slit him open like the first, with the man's innards dropping down in front of his face. The man could hardly breath, he was screaming for air and jerking his head all around trying to get air to his nose. His hands were tied together at the wrists, behind his back. Eventually he figured out that he could arch is neck back some, allowing his nose to be pointed to the ground but at least in the open air. Really, I do not know why he tried to stay alive so much. He had to know he was going to die. Charlie again took up a seat, having the fire lit with just the right intensity to see the man clearly, but not too bright. There was an opossum come by, right after dark, nipping and tugging at the man's innards, so close to his face, I think the thought of the animal biting into his face caused him more concern than the innards laying on the ground did. He would jerk and yell at the animal, trying to scare it off I suppose. It was not long though, before a pack of coyotes showed up, about eight in all. They would come in and out of the light, close to the man, on occasion stopping to sniff and look, then disappear in the dark again. Eventually two came in, taking nips at the innards, then jerking away with some in their mouth, thereby pulling on the man making him yell out. With the two pulling, as they started to growl, three more came in, grabbing innards as well, pulling and tugging. On occasion one would rip a piece loose, jerking its head back and swallowing it down, then back in for more. I did not look at Charlie. I was scared he may notice my lack of appreciation for what was happening and hang me too. Almost immediately after the last three showed, another came in, joining in pulling the innards. The man was jerking and being jerked as they pulled to rip pieces off. Enough of the man's innards had been pulled away and eaten by this time, that the man's face and upper chest were visible. Within a minute or so after the last one, another showed up, this one being rather large and husky, my guess a big male. The big coyote came alongside the man, who was screaming and yelling, still jerking and very much alive, which I could not believe, but he was. This big one, started to growl, showing his teeth, then lunged forward towards the man's neck like a bullet. Those jaws grabbed the man in the front center of the neck, clamping down like a vice. Almost instantly, blood spurted out from around the coyote's mouth, pumping in spurts with each beat of the man's heart, out through the dogs clenched jaws. The man was yelling just before the coyote grabbed him, so he was trying to inhale to get air in his lungs, through the jaws of the coyote. The teeth puncturing not only the main blood tube through the neck, but the air tube as well. As the man forcefully struggled to inhale, not only was some air getting in through his mouth, but the air was being sucked through the holes in his air tube, through the blood flowing out of his neck. It was a horrible, sucking, gurgling sound. With the exhale, the air came out through the same holes, through the blood, mixing it into a white froth like foam around the coyote's mouth, as well as the saliva of the coyote mixing in too. The man did not get a second inhale. With the coyote sensing the man could breathe, the animal did not let go, but tensed his body to help hold his grip, pressing down harder with his jaws. Blood was pouring out the man's nostrils and mouth, with bubbles forming, as there was still some breath but not much, as the breathing tube must have been completely closed with the extra pressure from the coyote. The man was trying to breath in, with his head and chest jerking with each attempt. It was just seconds after that the man was dead. After a short time of no struggle, the big coyote let go his grip, looked around his surroundings, then started to eat at the man's neck. The other coyotes joining in.

"Then I noticed Charlie. He was standing on his feet. So excited, the likes of which I had never seen him before. He swung his arms up, out into the air giving out a verbal victory holler, like he just won a battle or something. The coyotes looked up at us briefly, but sensing no danger to them, went back to feeding. I was embarrassed that I got so caught up in paying attention to what was happening to the man, that I did not even notice Charlie stand, nor did I think about him for those moments. He was looking around at the faces of others, with an open mouth grin from ear to ear, looking I believe for others to be sharing in his excitement. At that moment Charlie wanted camaraderie I believe. Quickly I turned away from Charlie, walking towards the dark on the other side of camp, so he could not see any dismay on my face. Charlie finally laid down for the night, whistling a cheery tune, as he lay his bedroll out. Could not get to sleep myself, with those coyotes, feasting themselves on a man, just yards away. Just after laying down, they must have been gnawing on his hands, because the cracking and crunching of bones was the loudest, even though his hands were tied behind his back, but I did not want to look. That could be me or anybody I thought. Oh, I was so ashamed at that moment. Charlie does not miss much, even in his excitement; as the next morning, Charlie made a comment to Ben, that maybe I was not appreciative of the evening's events. Ben made an excuse for me, telling him that blood made me a little weak kneed, which is how I ended up at the livery. Back in town, Charlie told me he did not want me riding with him any longer, with Ben telling me to take over the livery, as it is something I can definitely do well. As I look at it, I owe Ben my life. There are more than me riding with Charlie, that are still alive because of Ben's words. Ben is not blood thirsty like Charlie. Ben is the normal one, caught up in the center of abnormal men around him and over him. Ben is not a hero though, as neither am I, because a hero would have already killed Charlie, moving us all onto a different, more enlightened path."

"Why was Charlie not with Ben this day?" Maqoom asked.

"About six months ago, three wagons rode into town. Two horse team pulling each one, a man and woman on each one, along with five young ones between them all, along with a man riding a horse. They pulled up to the supply store, with not all of them even dismounted yet, when a young girl of about 15 or so, jumped off the first wagon, straight up the steps heading to the store. She was excited to see the store and to get in there. She was carrying a smile, with her eyes being bright, wide and alive. I was on the boardwalk, somewhat behind Charlie and the other guys. This girl was so hypnotizing to look at, I mean she was that attractive, that I was just plain staring and do not even know if I was breathing. This girl gave the word attractive its meaning, to grab a hold of you and hold you, you not wanting to look away. Do not know if I would say beautiful, but definitely she was attractive. Charlie did not hesitate. It even took me by surprise, how quickly he pounced upon this situation. These people did nothing wrong to him. He did not know any of them and they did not know him. At this point, it is my thinking that Charlie believes he is a king of old, with total supremacy, doing whatever he likes with no one to answer to. As the girl passed by him to go into the store, he reached out and caught her by the inside of her elbow. He forcefully spun her around, swinging her towards one of the men behind him, stating, 'take her to the house.' At the girls scream, the father was immediately telling Charlie to 'let my daughter go,' heading towards Charlie with a purposeful walk. Charlie pulled out his pistol, shooting the man, center in the chest. The man had one foot on the step, bringing the other foot up when the bullet hit him, pushing him back, making him hit the ground hard. The woman, whom I suppose was his wife, half climbed and half jumped off the wagon, screaming the man's name, kneeled down beside her husband and picked up his head, crying and sobbing, glancing at Charlie once or twice. Charlie half turned around to those around him and said, 'Shoot them all!' The guns come out blazing, with the man on the horse being the first one shot, as he was the only real threat, for he was armed and drawing his pistol. When the shooting stopped, there was not one of them alive, except the first girl with two horses getting hit too. They gathered up the bodies, taking them to a rock gorge some miles from town, where they threw them over the side to land in the rocks and bake in the sun. Eleven humans shot in cold blood, with another enslaved, without a wince of mercy being shown. Wanted so much to get on a horse, leaving this town, never coming back. But I knew Charlie would hunt me down, with the thought of what he would do to me after catching me, being more terrifying than the trauma of having to witness what just occurred in front of me. I did not pull my gun, which was the greatest rebellion I could think of mustering at that point against Charlie, as even that could cost me my life, but I was too scared to go through the act.

"Say about five days ago, one of Charlie's newest hands, decided to steal away with the girl. They got two days lead, before Charlie found out, so Charlie has been gone three now. The young man who took the girl does not stand a chance. He and her will be found and I for one, am glad that I do not have to see what Charlie will do to him. The girl will probably be brought back alive, but that man will sorely wish he had not made this decision. Ah! It almost makes me shiver, thinking how Charlie will make that man hurt before allowing him to die. Suspect I do, based upon past experiences, Charlie and the men will be back in maybe two more days. Imagine Ben is heading towards him now, to tell him of you."

Chapter 16
The Plan

With that, Maqoom got up out of the chair, walked into the livery, picking up his rifle, saddle bag and rope. He did not say a word to the livery man. No use putting him in any more danger than he is. He wanted more rope, but did not want to ask, knowing Charlie would be told everything he has with him. Two pistols, a rifle, saddle bag and rope. He could see in his mind, Charlie trying to figure out what the rope was for, but he was hoping that it would be a trifle point to Charlie, thereby letting it go; Maqoom knowing already what he had in store.

Ben Henson would be the first to die. He had plenty of opportunity to kill Charlie, preventing such horrible deaths, but he did not. Maqoom wanted Charlie Brandt wild. Not controlled. Like a wild beast that has been caged, losing all control of its senses, except the drive to be free. He wanted Charlie slashing out at everyone and everything. He walked out the same road he traveled in on. As he walked, thinking of what he was going to attempt to do, he was conscious that maybe he was a little too eager for this. Maybe his desire to kill Charlie was too personal, maybe even vengeful for those fellow humans who died so viciously and unnecessarily. He thought of the scripture, where those who '…shed man's blood, by man shall your blood be shed.' He was not thinking of Charlie as he thought this, but of himself. He had already killed so much up to this point, but it all seemed justified, at least to him as of this moment. He did not want to cross over, to separate from his Divine Maker, for any reason, let alone for hate or vengeance. Charlie could not be allowed to keep killing so freely. If it was the will of the Heavenly Court, that Charlie should be the victor, then so be it. But, Maqoom could not see it that way in his current state. Why would that scenario be allowed? Maqoom did not know the answer to that. But even if it went that way though, Maqoom was not going to question Divine Judgement. He would accept wholeheartedly. His largest concern was the possibility of his decision being wrong, hence the catalyst in pulling him away from closeness with the Creator. He owned nothing, he owed everything that he had in his possession, as well as his life, his very being to the Creator; with his desire to nourish a proper relationship with the Creator, the most important point of his life.

Maqoom kept walking along though, intent on pursuing the plan, keeping the thoughts and questions forefront, just in case he would get a glimpse of some concept or idea that would cause him to change his mind. It was always a concern of his, not just now, but always, that he not fall into the belief that he was well watered, when in reality he was spiritually dying of thirst. Separated from the Divine, by his own free will, with mixed up thoughts, feelings and emotions, the latter three all pulling their sustenance from the Tree of Knowledge of Good and Evil. That almost made him shudder, almost made him cry, as there was nothing more important in life as far as Maqoom was concerned, except to be as close to the Divine as the Divine Will decreed. He wanted to partake of the Tree of Life, not the other tree. He was a man of flesh and bone, with an eternal spirit within him, from the Creator. That spirit had direct connection with God, but sometimes his own flesh would get in the way, with the connection getting so unclear. He remembered what was written in Ecclesiastes, "Fear God and keep God's commandments, for that is a person's entire duty." He did fear God, he hoped he feared God, he was still working on it. He was going to continue his current path, on the grounds that it was just; to save any possible future people's lives from such cruelty and death. Not only future people, but their future generations after them as the Creator would allow. But please be attentive Maqoom, he thought to himself.

He physically stopped, closed his eyes and pointed his face up towards the sky. Tears were starting to form within them. He strived not to think of anything, nor hear anything, but just listen, just be. Striving to make contact with his Creator through the silence, the stillness of oneness, with all the superfluous inputs coming at him from all directions being ignored, pushed to the side, so he could be attentive. In the silence of nothingness, there one can possibly meet the Divine, he had been taught. After some minutes, he sensed he was calmer, he smiled opening his eyes. He openly said, "Thank You!" out loud, pointed his face down the trail and walked on.

Along the trail, he became fully aware of the sun burning against his temple and cheek area. It made him think of how powerful the Creator is, that the sun is so far away, yet it can burn the skin off a person, if the person would let it. Yet, the sun is a created object, like all the others out there he looks at on those clear nights, including the one he was walking on. As he approached the tree line, he noticed some wild blackberries along the one side. This reminded him of his mother, her taking him out in the woods for hours, going over what was edible and what was not, both of them carrying books she had bought from back East. He was so grateful for her, all the things she did for him, giving up of her own time and desires; she is indeed an inspiration to him and he is grateful to Heaven for her to be his mother.

After the scrumptious berry divergence, with his thanks being said, Maqoom headed into the woods along the trail. Some way, about 60 yards in, the road makes a slight bend to the left, just enough that one cannot see what is around the bend until making the turn. After clearing the bend, he stopped, surveying the right side of the road. About a hundred feet in, past the turn, there was a nice sapling on the right side, that was just over twice the size of his rope. He tested the young tree, determining it was sufficiently sturdy enough and tied his rope to it, a little higher than his own belt line. He ran the free rope down the tree, keeping it close, making a smooth turn at ground level, then running the rope across the road, over towards a much larger tree on the other side, some 30 feet from the roads edge. The opposing end of the rope was some ten feet short of him being able to comfortably conceal himself behind the big tree. Having some leather straps in his saddlebags, he found two appropriate saplings, took their two whip ends, bent them over each other and tied them together. Then he took the bigger end of the one, lined his rope up with it, approximately ten inches, wrapping the tag end around the tree and his rope, then tying it off with the leather strap. Maqoom, picked up the end of the second tree, and pulled. He pulled hard enough, that he was making the small tree on the other side of the road sway back and forth, with no seeming noticeable weak link in this rope tree combination. He allowed the rope to lay down, walking back to the other side, running the free rope down the small tree again, with a gentle bend at the bottom. Using his heel, he made a small furrow through the leaves and across the hard-packed trail. Then on his knees, using his hands, he covered and rustled the leaves over the rope, working to make sure it did not look like a piled-up line of leaves, then doing the same with the dirt across the trail. On his side, he covered the rope there as well, with the tag end laying on the ground, just behind the bigger tree he picked for concealment. Walking out to the opening again, but not in full view, he scanned the area between him and town, not noticing any movement, he walked down the trail towards his rope. As he cleared the bend, he was scanning, looking for any mistakes, but it looked appropriate to him. He knew where the rope lay, but it all looked appropriate, natural. Now he waits. If Charlie is who he has heard him to be, then he will be coming.

It was mid-afternoon on the second day. Maqoom was standing close to the tree where the tag end of the rope was close by. He was listening to the sounds of the forest and for the beat of horse's hoofs to be hitting the earth. Very glad he was, because of so much time that his mother took to walk the forest with him, each with a different book in their hands, learning about what is edible and what is not. Hours they would spend in search of edibles, sometimes whole days. Blackberries, wild carrots, wild celery and Mushrooms. He did not want to shoot any game, as he wanted them in the town to believe he was on the run for his life, in no way staying close to town.

He looked at his rope, making a mental note to pick up a second longer one, just in case it was required. There was a heavily worn deer trail, just yards from his location, that disappeared into a hole, in quite a substantial thicket of briers and vines, made by all the deer traversing into and out of it, over the years. Not wanting to disturb the plan he had laid out, he let his rope lay where it currently was. A second rope though, could be looped over the hole into the thicket, as the deer entered or exited the entrance their head would go through the loop. The rope would eventually tug on their chest, where at the feel of it they would bolt. Usually, with enough slack, they are running so fast that when it comes taut, it snaps their neck and there they lay. He could use some meat right now. It is better that he wait though he thought, because in his present situation, too much of the meat would go to waste before he could eat much.

With that he smiled, remembering one of the more pleasant times he and his father had together. They were out in early Fall, looking for deer sign, in preparation for gathering in meat for the winter. His dad said he had to go relieve himself, where a nice size tree had fallen, almost perfectly horizontal was its trunk, and about three foot off the ground. So, his dad walked over, with Maqoom looking the other way, when out of the sweet sounds of the forest, there came the sharp, jarring sound of a rattlers tail, from the direction of his Father. Just as Maqoom was debating whether to turn around his Father yelled out, "Shoot! Shoot Malcom!"

Maqoom turned, where he saw his father with his legs drawn up so that his feet were almost level with the underside of the tree trunk. His pants were down around his ankles and directly under him, but slightly on the far side of the tree was the biggest rattler he had seen to date, coiled, with its head up in the center, ready to strike. Tail just a firing off. His dad yelled again, "Shoot boy!"

Maqoom had his rifle in his hands, of which he thought he was a fairly good shot with, but this was shooting directly under his father and if he was shaky or missed, he could hit or kill his own father. Maqoom could sense he was starting to quiver within himself, just as his Father yelled, "Shoot!"

The quivering went away, the gun came up and just as he was taught by his dad and had practiced, the sites were where the bullet was to hit, Maqoom squeezed the trigger. The head of the rattler basically disappeared, being thrown back by the impact. The rattling stopped its intensity, so his dad grabbed his pants, pulling them up at the same time as jumping down and off from the tree trunk. When he got beside Maqoom, he finished buttoning up and cinching his belt. They both turned facing the tree, fully assured that the ratter was dead, but still squirming and rattling slightly from its death throes. They walked over to look at the sight, realizing what actually occurred, his dad had defecated directly on top of the rattler, hitting it square on the head. No wonder, that was one ticked off rattler. Maqoom's shot was square on the lower jaw, splitting the head, basically completely sheering one side of its head from its body. His dad looked at him, giving him one of the few positive verbalizations that Maqoom could remember. "Nice shot son!"

Maqoom, smiled at the thought. Life could have been so much different, but: He stopped his thoughts, virtually shaking his mind, as if to shake off where he was going with those thoughts and get back to where he was.

God gives to everyone exactly the information and opportunities for success. Success being defined as achieving a oneness with the Creator that the Creator wants for a person, in the time span that the Creator gives that person, in this physical realm of existence.

He thought about King David, how the King was not

allowed to build the Temple. At one point, when he was much younger, he thought maybe King David shed to much blood. But then as he got older, he read of the concept, that because of all the blood that was shed under King David's authority, that if King David built the Temple, then the Creator would not be able to justify destroying the Temple as punishment to the nation, if such an act would ever be necessary. All the blood shedding was done under the strict Authority of Heaven, for the sake of Heaven; such that the Temple would have to stand forever. Hence, it would have to be his son, who was brought to the throne through a peaceful transition of power, who would build the Temple.

Maqoom had heard of two different sheriffs, both of whom could efficiently kill and both of whom the townspeople adored. One who all the townspeople talked up as the most righteous man they knew or had ever known; the other known as a good man, yet both of these sheriffs died by the hand of man. Yet King David was allowed to die a natural death. He was not killed by another human. President George Washington too, was allowed a natural death. Maybe King David and President George Washington never killed outside of what the Creator willed. Killing with no malice nor hatred, but only killing as necessary, out of a sense of kindness for their fellow humans, wanting them to be free, out from under tyranny. Killing out of a sense of justice, to remove those who do not fear the Creator, to remove those who so flagrantly abuse their fellow humans. Killing out of a sense of righteousness, as it is right to strive to help bring morality and freedom to ones fellow humans. To kill with these concepts being the foundation of the fight, means that there was indeed a relationship with the Divine. Some people clearly know of the attachment with the Creator, some people not so much. But as you study King David and President George Washington, one can be sure that their spirits were connected with the Creator of spirits. Their killings done with the consciousness that they were picked to carry out the Divine Plan.

Maqoom thought about the number of people he had killed so far, in such a young life. He remembered his anger back in town when he was facing the cowboy in the street. He believed he had already failed when he remembered that. He thought of the scripture verse again, '…shed man's blood, by man shall your blood be shed.' He looked up to the sky, such a deep blue, so expansive; the blue of course directing out one's thoughts to the Throne of God. He does not want to murder. Killing is one thing, but murder is another. He does not want to be separated from his Creator, as unity with God is the purpose of life. He verbalized, to the Court of Heaven, apologizing for his lack of knowledge, certainty, on what he has been doing and on the ramifications of killing people. To kill someone is to take all the generations that would come after them too. There was a slight shudder within Maqoom, at the thought of not knowing how many people will not be born, for every person he has killed or will possibly kill. He will not know that until he crosses over himself, changing his garments, going over to the other side. Per his current understanding level, he did not consider any of those he had killed to be murder. Fully realizing he had anger with the one in the street, he resolved within himself to get control of that. He asked for guidance to do what is kind, just and righteous. He said "Amen," lowering his head to look at the road, his rope, his gun and thinking about his plan.

It is frustrating sometimes to be so corpulent, yet it is

so grand to be alive and human. To have to struggle with the inappropriate mixing of that which should not be mixed, a result of his sin in the Garden. Maqoom had read that before the sin, we were perfectly balanced, between physical body and spirit, translucent in our appearance. But after the sin, we became out of balance, with physicality seemingly to appear as if it is dominant; our beings appearing very corpulent. But, the balance can be restored in this life, if a human desires and works at it; with the help of the Creator. He does not ever blame Adam in his thoughts, but always himself, as he cannot say that he would have done any differently.

His thoughts now turned back to his current, physical situation. There was enough water to last through tomorrow, but after that he would have to go for water. He did not want to leave during the day, thinking the gang would not ride at night. If this was going to work, he would have to go for water after sunset.

Chapter 17
The Song

After a nice meal of berries, carrots and mint greens to top it off, he walked along the edge of the road to the opening. He should have been watching ahead more than he was watching the ground for victuals. As he sensed he should look up, doing so, he immediately saw the posse, almost a quarter of the ground between him and town traversed by them. He quickly jumped into the forest, straining through the leaves to see if they showed any sign of noticing him. Their path did not veer, nor did they halt or slow their forward progress. There were quite a few of them, more than 12 for sure, but he did not take time to count. Heading back through the forest, he got to his tree and rope. Both pistols loaded, rifle loaded and leaning against the tree, it was time.

Maqoom wanted Ben Henson first. As he had contemplated previously, he wanted Charlie Brandt wild, not controlled, so Ben had to be taken out of the way. Like a wild animal that has been caged, losing all control of its senses, except the drive to be free. Slashing out at everyone and everything. Charlie would actually be helping Maqoom at that point, to eliminate the band of thugs. Maqoom had grappled with that thought, over the past days. The plan was to eliminate the whole group. Who was he, to actually have the intent to carry out such a plan, as to wipe out a whole group of people? The doubts of his own will, in trying to carry out this plan started to flood his thinking, but he forcefully pushed them out. He did not sense that his desire to carry out this plan was based upon thoughts, feelings nor emotions; but on his desire for kindness, justice and righteousness towards his fellow humans that desired such lives, to live in peace and harmony with their fellow humans. This was the plan and he had the intent to carry it out, as best as possible. Hopefully, with the Court of Heaven on his side, the plan would be successful. How many lives would be spared, he thought; how many screams of torment and anguish would never take place, how much unjust spilt blood would the earth not have to forcefully swallow, with the elimination of this group?

As the first horses entered the boundary of the forest Maqoom's senses changed. It was like the sun coming up over the horizon, lighting everything, no shadows; but it was all happening in his brain, his soul. He was calm. Maybe even calmer than he was that morning in the woods, with the sounds and the smells so pleasant.

His hearing amplified, as he heard sounds that were not there seconds before. Insects calling, birds chirping, squirrels rummaging through the forest floor and scampering among the treetops above. The squirrel's nails scratching and breaking bark as they traversed from place to place. The horse's hoofs contacting the compacted earth of the road. He caught himself, trying to count how many horses there were from the hoof beats, but let it go when what he was trying to calculate hit his conscious level. Horses blowing, as they were curious and unsure of entering the forest. A man clearing his throat, another man sneezed.

His sight broadened. He was seeing more, all at the same time. Between his central vision and peripheral vision, the shadows got lighter, the colors more vibrant. Looking straight ahead, he was so aware of many different butterflies, that he did not notice before. His brain counted six, without even looking at them, nor did he ask his brain to do so. The number presented itself in his brain, like a deer materializes in the forest, where he was not, just seconds before. He saw branches move with the slightest breeze, leaves swaying with the caress of the breeze. He did not even realize seconds before that there was a breeze. Now he felt it across his cheek skin, coming from the southeast, still cool from the evening air. He also felt patches of heat from the rising, angled rays of the sun, that which filtered through the canopy, onto the side of his face and neck. Even his skin was more alert, he thought to himself. His sense of touch was so strong, he was thinking he could sense his own skin. Like his mind was clearly knowledgeable of every square inch of his body as well as everything outside his body that presented any type of input to his brain. He almost allowed what was about to occur, that which he had planned for, to leave his mind. So engrossed was he in what was happening to him and the pleasantness of being so involved with the creation, so one, that he did not want to lose it.

Life was singing their songs to the Creator. Each created object, earth, moon, stars and universe, each doing their assigned tasks. The trees, leaves, breeze, butterflies, squirrels and insects all doing what they were created to do. All culminating in a crescendo of song towards the One Who made them, by their all doing what they were created to do. Only man was missing from this song, at this moment. The one who had the free will to choose to obey or to disobey the Creator. If man would join in, doing that which man is to do, following the Will of the Creator, then the song would be complete. Reaching the very heavens, causing the angels to rejoice and sing praise to the Creator. With the one who has free will, choosing to join in the song of Creation, completing the oneness of Creation with the Creator, then the purpose of Creation is achieved, with the whole universe being affected, all serving the Creator as one, being one with the Creator.

Now, now he had an intellectual grasp of why a butterfly flapping its wings on the other side of the planet, being joined by all the other creation doing their parts, coming together with a human or humans singing their songs of obedience too, how all that obedience, culminating together can affect positively the whole of creation, on this planet and throughout space and the heavens. He was one with everything and everything was one with him, with the joy of the connection with the Creator being so overpowering, that he had a sense like he had no gravity pushing against him, like he was weightless. He was a part of the whole, though a leading part in completing the whole. He realized then that the disobedience can affect the whole as well, tearing at the fabric of creation, affecting the whole negatively. In this current realm of existence, he realized there has to be balance between the good and the bad, until at some point, everyone will turn to the good in obedience to the Creator.

It was to him, within his mind, that the acquiring by the brain of all the input from the senses, along with the spiritual concepts that were opening to his awareness, the physical brain and the spirit within him, were presenting a picture to him, of a full circle around him, including himself. The relative directions of left, right, forward, backward, up and down were concepts that seemed to be transforming into absolutes. His awareness of where he was in space, compared to everything else around him was firm within his mind, even as it changed from moment to moment. Everything else was changing, but he was staying the same, even as he moved as well. The thought crept up to his consciousness that maybe he could even close his eyes, and still be fully aware of everything around him, but he pushed that out as the eyes were so much involved with the input to the brain. But his soul was involved too. He did not know how for sure, but he knew that it was. So blissful was he at this moment, so one with the creation, that if one of the men's horses had not given out a blow, he might have allowed the whole gang to ride by without him doing anything. He did not want to leave where he was! But, the horse blew, just as the first rider was making the turn onto the straightway, heading to the rope.

None of the inputs left him. He was fully aware, both internally and externally, knowledgeable of all that he had been picking up before that last horse blow. There was no anger, no fear, no anxiety. He had heard of people in fights, getting narrow sighted, not fully seeing the enemy standing before them, but only aware of a certain percentage of the whole. Also, how their hearing shuts down, as they tell of not hearing anyone nor anything, until after they realize they have survived the event. But what he had right now was so opposite of that, he was grateful within himself for what was happening. In the process leading up to reigning terror upon the earth, he was grateful within himself, to the Divine, for all that was happening.

Charlie Brandt's horse was a nose ahead of any other. Ben Henson was on Charlie's right, with a man on Charlie's left, along with a second man further left. The four were fairly lined up with Charlie as the point of the spear. Maqoom allowed all four to cross the rope. Next in line were three men. The ones on each side were slightly ahead of the man in the middle, by about a horse's neck. When the horses under the two men on each side had both front feet over the rope, Maqoom pulled hard. The rope held and even better, the connection to the tree branches held firm as well. Maqoom could see within his mind the whole group as one beast so to speak, a beast with 36 appendages, any one of which could be a harm to him. The number of men now being known to him, even though he did not consciously count them.

The earth, small pieces of bark, grains of sand, leaves and other materials ground into fine particles from the horse's hoofs and wagon wheels, which had traversed this path throughout the years, came up with the rope. The rope physically hit the two side horses just behind their front legs onto their brisket. That was enough to break their current lulled state as they plodded along. Add in the particles of earth and such that hit too and them horses went berserk. Both side horses went straight up like a kangaroo. They bowed their backs like a cat stretching or a broncing horse trying to throw off the imposition that was on its back. The rider farthest across from Maqoom was riding well, staying on his horse, riding out the rampage. The rider closest to Maqoom, did not fare as well. His horse was lighter and wiry. It cleared the ground well over two feet, straight up, with the rider nowhere ready for such an event. The rider flew off the horse, coming down hard on his left hip, elbow then shoulder. Maqoom heard bone or bones breaking, ligaments snapping, whatever it was; it was not pleasant, as the man's groan hushed the forest.

The middle horse went straight up off its front feet.

The particles of debris hitting it under the neck and on its chest, as well as the rope just glancing it across the upper part of its front legs, made it act as if some of the small particles of debris were actually ground up pieces of teeth from a Velociraptor, that was forming back into a whole creature, rising out of the earth to sink its teeth into its neck. It brought its front legs straight up. The rider not thinking correctly, held tight to the reigns, with the straighter the horse getting, the tighter the rider held on. As the rider was losing his seat, the weight of his body pulled the horses head back further and to one side. The rider landed on his feet, but his legs were not prepared, so he went down hard on his butt. The horse came over, directly on top of him, as if it dropped out of the air on its side. The impact so crushed the man, Maqoom heard the man's ribs breaking, as well as a large expansive exhale of breath coming out of the man, as his chest was crushed by the gravitational force pushing on the mass of the horse.

Ben Henson was too close to Charlie to turn his horse left, nor did he want to twist in his saddle as Charlie Brandt and the other two men did. Ben swung his horse to the right, away from Maqoom, so as to swing it around to face this interloper. As Ben acquired Maqoom in his sights, his eyes and face showed the signs of recognition, as his mind realized they rode into a trap. Since Ben only carried one side arm, he had to take the time, though ever so slight, but enough, to toss his reigns into his left hand. As he was swinging his arm back for the revolver, Maqoom lifted his left hand and squeezed off a shot. The slug hit Ben Henson on the bridge of his nose. As the projectile pushed into his head, the energy from the impact initially bulged is eyes out even more than they already were. Just briefly though, as the slug made it into the soft matter of the brain, the eyes went back to where they were, wide eyed, but not bulging. The speed of the bullet along with the friction against the brain material, pulled brain matter with it. It was not just burrowing through the brain but was pushing along that which was in front of it and pulling along that which it rubbed against. The bullet exited the upper back of the skull, making a hole not much larger than the projectile, but jagged. Maqoom saw the funnel shape of brain material with small pieces of skull intermixed, escaping through the hole, dissipating as it spread out, being stopped by the friction with the air and pushed down by gravity. The wetness of the material reflected the rays of the sun, making the material glisten ever so slightly, more than it would have on its own. The skull also cracked into a couple pieces. One piece flew up and forward, being held to the head by the skin, as it acted like a hinge. Maqoom saw the section stand straight up, like Ben's hair decided to make this rectangular shape, but it was the skull under it, with the hair going along. Ben had a tight hold on his reigns too, bringing his horse up off its front legs, as Ben slid backwards in the saddle. As Ben's body relaxed, the reigns were let loose, but the horse had traveled up high enough, that Ben fell back off the rump of the horse, landing flat on his back, with the sound of a thump, when a mass hits an immovable object. As the horse was coming back down with its front legs, Ben's legs, which were bent at both the hips and the knees, over stretched as the sudden impact with the earth stopped the torso, but not the legs. As soon as the leg and thigh muscles had stretched as much as they were going to, because of the overstretching, the legs shot straight out, with such force it tugged at the torso. Ben's left foot touched the horse's left back hoof, just as the horse's front hoofs were contacting the ground. The horse shot out of the hole like a bullet out of a barrel.

Charlie Brandt yelled at his horse, kicking it hard in its sides. He laid down flat on the saddle, leaning to the right to try to protect his body with the horse. Maqoom saw then what type of man Charlie Brandt really was. Charlie had no intent to face this, he was running. The two to Charlie's left kicked their horses too, with all three racing down the road.

The closest man, who lay on the ground was going for his pistol. Even in the tremendous pain that he was in, as his movement and contorted face shown, he still had the wherewithal to go for his gun. Maqoom shot him with his left hand as well. Hitting the man in the nostrils, his head was only inches from the ground as he laid there. The slug threw his head down hard, against the ground. As his head impacted the earth, with nowhere else to go, the energy of the slug upon his head, had to dissipate throughout his physical matter and as it did, it slightly pulled on the shoulders of the man's body. Then he was relaxed.

Ben's horse had turned back towards town, racing back between the far bucking bronco rider and the middle man who lie, crushed on the earth. It raced wild back through the trailing men, hitting one horse so hard, pressing against the rider's leg, that the rider cussed a whirlwind at the disappearing horse, almost forgetting there was a shooter, extremely close by. Just as the trailing riders were getting some control on their nervous animals, the wild run of Ben's horse commenced the turmoil all over again amongst the animals. Riders having to get control again.

The bronco rider on the far side was getting control over his beast, when Maqoom took him with his left hand, catching him in the temple, literally blowing both eyes out of their sockets, as the bullet hit the left outer eye socket bone, through the back of both eyes, breaking the eye socket bone on the other side. The man slid off the right side of his horse, like he had grease between him and the saddle.

The horse of the middle man had managed to get itself on all fours, immediately racing back through the trailing men. This path slightly different than Ben's horse had taken but causing just as much chaos and keeping the other horse's jittery and almost at their wits end. The horse's noses were flaring, their heads and tails held high. Some were squealing, others were trumpeting, with all but one prancing and extremely agitated. Their riders constantly fighting to get them to not follow the other two back to town.

Maqoom then took two of the closest men further back, with his right hand. The one in front and then the one behind. Two shots, with hardly a separation of time between them. Both men hit in the head, the first man took his in the ear canal, with body material splatting against the man to his right, whom was now, not only having to fight his horse, but he had to close his eyes as the spray of brain splatted the right side of his face. The man behind took his bullet just below the nose, shattering the man's upper jaw, with a couple of his upper teeth falling on the man's saddle. The spray from that man's brain material, catching the rider behind and to the right of him, directly in the face, with the used bullet passing so close to the farthest riders head in the back of the pack, that he heard it slice through the air going by him, jerking his head away from where the sound came from. Immediately the man swung his horse around to his right, kicking its sides and yelling out. The horses from the latest two hit, went opposite directions. The forward one ran forward, chasing the horse of the man in front of him. The back riders horse turned back, towards town.

Two other riders in the back now swung their horses around, they too kicking their horse's sides, fervently striving to get away from what was happening. It is possible they did not even see Maqoom, as the tree branches might have covered him somewhat from their direct sight, but Maqoom could see them clearly.

The man that was sprayed in the face with his riding buddy's brains was calming down and going for his gun. He looked angry. The fear gone, replaced with anger. Maqoom wanted to take him, but there was another, closer who was on the inside, riding just behind the man whose horse had crushed him, he was already drawing his gun.

Maqoom took that man with his right hand, then the farther back, angry man too with the same gun. It was slightly a farther distance between them, than the last two, but the time between shots was not noticeable to the average human ear. The closer of the two, looking more forward towards Maqoom, took his bullet on his left eyebrow. This caused his head to jerk to the left, almost spinning him out of the saddle, as he fell on the ground face first. The next man, farther back, had his gun cleared of the holster, but still pointing to the earth. As Maqoom swung on him, the man fired with the bullet hitting the ground next to his horse's hoof, causing his horse to jump sideways to the left. Maqoom's bullet caught him directly in his right eye. With no real resistance to its travel from the soft tissue of the eye in the front, it busted through the back of the eye socket, into the brain pan, bursting forth with a spray of mist glistening in the angled rays of the sun, exiting just behind his right ear. Falling back off his horse on the right side, he landed hard on the earth, but he was dead, not feeling a thing as he hit.

The next man was also somewhat behind the crushed man, but farther over away from Maqoom. He was turning his horse towards town without any indication he was going for a gun. The man behind him though, was intending to fight, gun cleared and coming up, Maqoom took him with the right hand also, catching him with the slug on the bridge of his nose too. This man though was tensed, angry and spoiling for a fight. The slug caught him, jerking his head back, the man's arms raised up in the air with his hands above his head. The gun flew forward with the momentum of the curve of the man's hand, and the loss of grip from the man's death, it flew through the air, past the man that was heading for town, with the gun going one direction and the rider and horse the opposite direction. The next got about three gallops, almost to where the latest victim lay, when Maqoom caught him just behind his right ear, this time with his left hand. The bullet traveling through the brain, coming out in front of the man's left ear. Because of the forward thrust of his horse, the momentum carried the man in his death as if he was diving off a cliff headfirst, hands out forward. He hit the ground, with first contact being his chest. Skidding slightly across the ground, he came to a stop. The horse never slowed.

With the back three already moving fast out of the area, that meant two remaining. The farthest two across the trail. The back one seemed paralyzed, he was looking at his horse, the horse was looking at Maqoom. The man in front of him, had finally had enough of his wild horse, and was getting down to make his stand on his feet. At least that is a fighter Maqoom thought. Maqoom took the sitting man with his right hand gun, throwing the projectile in his left ear, with the bullet coming out the top part of his right ear. The man slid out of the saddle, in the direction of the bullet, with the horse barely budging from its position. Even in the midst of battle, Maqoom did not like what he just did, but this man rode with Charlie. He chose his side to ride on and now his ride ended. The last man was on the ground, turned and facing Maqoom. His revolver was already out of its holster and moving forward towards Maqoom. Maqoom swung his left hand gun onto the man, just as the man prematurely fired with the bullet catching the earth to the left and out in front of Maqoom. Maqoom's slug caught the man in the left nostril, pushing through his brain, exiting the lower part of the back of his skull. The horse immediately bolted when the rider was off, so the bullet hit the trees behind the man. Maqoom could hear it ripping though the green leaves, then thumping and burying itself into wet wood.

Eleven dead, seven alive. Three one way, three another and one laying on the trail in front of him, gasping for air, maybe knowing he was dead, maybe not. Maqoom took his left gun, raised it and fired. Taking the man with his slug just below his left earlobe, coming out the other side, burying itself in the packed dirt of the trail.

All alive were gone except for the horse under the paralyzed man. It had started to eat the grass along the edges of the trail. That was the calmest horse Maqoom had ever witnessed. Maqoom removed the spent cartridges, loading fresh bullets in all chambers. Closing the cylinders of each gun, he kept them down at his sides, in his hands. He stood there listening, looking out over the bodies.

Charlie noticed the shots had ceased, so he stopped his horse. The two men following stopped theirs as well.

They were just listening. The two men had never seen Charlie run before and it unnerved them some, as well as disgusted them some too. Neither would share with each other what they were thinking and absolutely not share it with Charlie, as he might shoot them right there. They never saw Charlie get ambushed either, so this whole experience was new to them. After a few minutes, Charlie nudged his horse forward, with the other two following. They were circling around, heading back to town.

Maqoom placed the revolvers in their respective holster, walked past the tree his rifle was leaning against, pulled the rifle up to himself and walked toward the clearing and a view of the town. He had made a path in the forest, over the past two days, so as to be able to get to the clearing to see towards town, without having to use the main wagon trail. He saw the three men who rode back towards town, stopped some 300 yards away. They seemed to be in an argument of sorts. Maqoom catching a piece of loud voice on occasion, with wild gestures from the men using their arms and hands.

Two of the three wanted to go back, kill whoever had done this and find Charlie. They were terrified Charlie would kill them for leaving him. The other argued that they could meet Charlie in town, as he would use the old miners trail to swing around, coming into town on the South side. Finally, in frustration the loner yelled out, "Charlie ran, why do we have to go back?"

This silenced the other two, who just looked at him. He knew immediately he should not have said that. One of the pair spoke up, "You are going to come with us or I will tell Charlie what you said."

The loner was stuck. He did not want to go, but he did not want to face Charlie either, even if he is a runner.

Charlie was much faster than him with a six gun, and much more deadly with one too. The man, exasperated, frustrated, angrily whispered out, "Ok."

The two turned their horses back towards the forest, with the loner's horse already pointing that way. They are coming back Maqoom could see, somewhat surprised they would. Maqoom slipped back his trail, cautiously watching, as he did not know where Charlie and the other two had went.

The awareness level had dissipated slightly, but it was still much higher than an average day. He made it back to his small clearing, paused a minute before crossing it, reached a large tree on the far side, turned and waited. He had a nice view of the trail, while at the same time he was somewhat covered by the overhead foliage and the tree trunk itself. As the first hoof on the earth, became a conscious thought to him, he was back to the earlier awareness level, as when he had started this fight. They were not walking their mounts in, they were running them in. The strategy did not make much sense, as they had no idea where he was or even sure how many there were. Maqoom knew they were scared and desperate. He did not know why they would come back, but here they were and he was not planning on wasting the opportunity. Constantly vigilant of everything happening full circle around him, he was ready. Two were coming in on Maqoom's right and one on the left side of the trail. All had their firearms in their hands, hammers cocked. As the first man commenced to rein his horse back, pistol out in front, weaving about like an owl's head, looking for a target to go after, Maqoom squeezed off a shot from his rifle. The slug punched the man square on his sternum, coming out just below the shoulder blade. The energy from the impact caused his shoulders to hunch forward, with his arms immediately starting to drop. The far left man squeezed off a shot, with the bullet hitting the ground at the base of the tree Maqoom stood behind. This man was running his horse full force through the dead men on the ground, from the earlier exchange. At one point his horse could not side step them all, stepping squarely on one, the exaggerated gait of the horse to keep his own balance, almost knocked the man off the horse, but he hung on. This occurred just as his second shot went off, hitting the tree Maqoom was behind. The gun from the man shot in the chest hit the ground, with the man's body not too far behind. After the bullet exited the first man, it then hit the next man square on his right shoulder joint, traveling from front to back at an angle, completely shattering the joint, making the man's right arm hang solely from ligaments, muscle and skin. He gave out a terrific yell, surprised by the fact he was hit. His gun too hit the ground within seconds of the first mans. Maqoom took this second one, with his next shot, square in the chest as well. The energy of the slug, throwing his upper body back, to where his shoulders hit the horse's haunches. This made the horse lunge, coming out from under the man who hit the ground on the back of his head, with his legs and shoulders in the air. He was already dead, but Maqoom heard the audible crack of his neck, as the back of the skull impacted the earth, with the mass of the body continuing down, snapping the neck bone like a branch.

The third, far left man fired off his third shot, even though he was past the tree Maqoom was standing behind. He was scared, just firing in a general direction, not really aiming at anything or anyone. Trying to pin Maqoom to his chosen spot, until he was far enough away to get clear of a bullet. Maqoom ran to the far side of the road, lining himself up with the path the man's horse was taking. With the front of the rifle on the back of the man's head, Maqoom squeezed the trigger. The rifle bullet caught the man square on his spine, burrowing holes through the man's intestines, exiting the muscle and skin of the stomach. It was not an instantly fatal shot, but totally smashed the man's spine. The bullet hit the horse in the meat of the neck, causing it to jump and kick with its back feet, while still in full gallop. Between the bullet relaxing the man and the kick and jump of the horse, the rider flew off the saddle to the left of the horse. At one point Maqoom could visualize the man riding in midair beside the horse, as the horse was to the man's right, while he was in a riding position in the air, saddle high. Gravity took hold quickly, with the man falling fast, hitting the ground on his butt. The friction of the earth against him, slowed that part down, but the upper torso and head kept going since the spine was severed. In the end, the man was sitting in the road, with his head swung forward, only inches from his knees, with only skin and muscle keeping him from folding in half.

Maqoom turned half around to his right. The relaxed horse was still there, head up looking straight at Maqoom. The horse of this last man shot could still be heard galloping strong. It disappeared around the next bend in the road, with Maqoom letting the sound of it dissipate, before he moved. Allowing the browsing horse opportunity to continue, Maqoom walked over to the clearing. Loading fresh bullets into the rifle, all weapons were at their max capacity. Finding a comfortable spot, he sat on the ground with his back against a tree. Other trees were between him and the road, but he had a clear line of site out over most of the bodies on the road. If anyone was sneaking up, the movements of the horse on the other side would be a distraction.

Chapter 18
Tranquility

When he awoke, he could not believe he had fallen asleep, nor how quickly it had happened. Everything was in its place, with the horse on his side of the road, under the canopy shade of the big tree, which Maqoom stood behind when the last three came riding in. It stood there with its head and neck drooped, eyes closed, ears relaxed, facing down the road towards town. Maqoom stayed motionless, so thankful that no one walked up and shot him sleeping. There was only three of the original remaining, of which he did not believe any of them would come back this way today. But, still somewhat embarrassed he had fallen asleep in such a situation, also somewhat agitated with himself for doing so. However, thankfully no one took him, so it was time to let it go and move on. Still he hesitated for a spell, listening and watching. The alert level he was at earlier had ceded, with him sensing he was at his normal, for him. He continued to watch and listen. The birds were somewhat quiet, it being the heat of the day. The horse was calm, but that did not speak much after what Maqoom witnessed with this horse. Earlier, the horse was calm through the whole episode. If it was not for the fact that his rider locked up in psychological paralysis, with such a calm horse, that rider would have been the most immediate danger to him after the first shot was fired off.

After being assured, as best as he could that no one was lining up a site on him, Maqoom raised up and stretched. The horse looked over at him. Maqoom walked over to the horse, raising up his hand and letting him smell it, then he rubbed its nose and forehead. Taking it by the reins, he led it back into the clearing somewhat farther from the road. It was time for a soak and to get some fresh water. If it would not have been for them riding out this morning, he would have had to head to the stream this evening anyway, as his drinking water would be out by sunset. He mounted the horse, with the horse being agreeable, giving him a little nudge with the heels of his boots, on the horse went. He liked this horse the more he was around it. Though he thought with a slight smile, if he ever had lead flying at him and the horse just prodded along, he definitely would no longer like the horse. Staying off the main road, he rode through the forest. He guessed it was a six or seven mile ride, with it being so thick three different times, that he had to walk the horse through. After covering the distance of where he thought would be the stream, he had to cover slightly more ground when he started to hear the gurgle of water over rocks.

As he got closer to the stream, he felt the coolness effect of the water upon the air, even though the shade of the trees was already cool, it was even more so close to the stream. Then there it was. Dismounting he walked along it for a time, finding the hole deep enough for his plans, he walked the horse into the stream below the hole, letting it drink and browse along its edges as it wished. He stripped down, going into the deeper hole with his clothes in his hands. It was almost as deep as he was tall. As he was walking in deeper, the coldness of the water was making him take short quick breaths, as the temperature was uncomfortable. Once he got chest deep, he bent his knees, going under. It was cold, but it was nice to have the water wash over him. Coming up, he almost hyperventilated, as he was taking such quick, short but deep breaths, his body trying to stay warm he guessed. For a time he just stayed there up to his neck, trying to get control of his breathing and let his body settle down some. The movement of the water across his skin, kept him at an uncomfortable temperature, so going under again, rubbing his hair with his shirt, he came up and got somewhat shallower, so he could sit with the water just over his belly button. Again, using his shirt as a washcloth, he rubbed his arms and the back of this neck. Not forgetting to get behind his ears, as his mother would tell him. The thought gave him a big smile, as he washed dutifully, even though Mother was not looking. Washing his pants, shirt and under garments, he took one more dunk, getting up to determine how to allow his garments to dry. After squeezing out the water as best as he could, he hung them over a branch along the bank. There was a slight breeze, but without the sun's rays, they would not dry out, but just be very cold and wet to put back on. Taking his two canteens, he went to the head of the hole, where the water was moving well and rippling, he filled them both.

Being that it was going to be dark soon, he did not want to spend the night here. Putting his britches on, gathering up the remaining clothes, he got on the horse, letting it walk up the stream. Based upon the fact that he noticed the stream some distance off, when he was first riding towards the town, he knew that the stream came through a sparsely treed area on the East side of the forest. His plan was to hunker down there for the night, wrapped in his dry bed roll. Let his clothes dry the next day in the sun, with the plan being to find some victuals and relax. It was just after full dark when the clearing opened before him. Even though the road was some ways off, he went up the far bank from the road, to find his spot. There was somewhat of a clear spot under a nice size pine tree, of which the limbs and needles would help to keep the dew off him. He hung all his clothes on a branch that would catch the morning rays of the sun, allowed the horse to graze freely, wrapped up in his blanket, closed his eyes and waited. His body was shivering quite seriously before he first wrapped up, but now it was getting warmer from his own body heat and the dry blanket wrapped around him. As the shivering was almost unnoticeable, sleep visited him.

He slept somewhat later than his usual. When he first opened his eyes, he realized the singing of a couple birds was actually in his last dream. As he came out of sleep, the songs of the birds in his dream, eased along with him into the realm of the awake. He was on his right side, facing the tree with the stream to his back. Listening for a time, being satisfied that the sounds seemed unalarming, he slowly rolled to his back to get a gaze out over the stream and in the direction of the road. His clothes were directly in the sun. The horse was over in the shade of an oak tree, head and neck still drooped from its doze, but eyes and ears on Maqoom. Laying there for some minutes, he finally got up, stretched and checked his clothing. The clothing was not dry yet. *Maybe just after noon*, he thought. Not wanting to walk around naked though, he did put on his long john bottoms and boots, to look for some food. He was famished. Finding all that he needed, he hung his johns back on the limb.

He was under the pine tree, sitting on his blanket, with the tag ends of the blanket overlapping, over his loins. He looked up saying a blessing to the Creator, acknowledging from Whom this food came from. He ate, chewing the food appropriately, not only to help digestion as his mother had told him, but to also enjoy the deliciousness of it as it was chewed allowing the taste buds time to pick up the nuances of the flavors, sending the interpreting signals for them to the brain. Chewing, not gulping also allowed the body the ability to acknowledge the satiety point, before overeating occurred. Drinking the water from the stream was just as satisfying as the food. Really clean, refreshing water it was. Looking up to the blue sky with the fluffy white clouds interspersed about and the flavor interpretations still linger in his consciousness along with the comfortable, satisfying felling of satiety, he gave his thanks to the Creator along with a smile.

He sat for some time. Listening to the birds, thinking about God and pondering all the life that was currently happening around him. Birds, frogs, crickets, a mama deer and her half- grown fawn. He thought about the events of yesterday and what led up to that point. Not coming to any conclusions about anything, but just thinking, pondering; being is what he was doing. After finding some more eats for lunch, drinking the clean water from the stream, he took another nap on his blanket, in the cool of the shade from the tree. Coming to again about mid-afternoon, he looked over at his clothes, thinking it is time to move on. The clothes were nice and dry. The horse was still there, browsing in the area, relaxed as ever. Putting the bit and bridle back on the horse, then saddling it up, he got himself in the saddle, ready to go. Getting back in the saddle changed his internal composition. Where he was, what seemed to him totally relaxed just a moment ago, now he was scanning with his eyes, listening with his ears, ready to draw at the slightest hint of something not right. Because of the riders that went to get Ben and how long it took for them to get back, Maqoom knew the direction and approximate distance of Charlie's house from town. He also could see in his mind, where he was in comparison to town. Having the information about the riders and the picture of where he was, he had an approximate idea of where Charlie's house was, as well as the direction to take to get there. He cut the horse away from the stream, heading through the forest, instead of taking the road or going into or close to town.

He was not in a hurry, nor was it fast going anyway, since there was no trail that he was following. On occasion he would cut a deer trail going his way and he would follow it, but invariably it would cut off in some direction he was not going. Sometime after midday, he cut a small feeder stream, that from its direction would cut into the larger stream he washed up in yesterday. Getting down off the horse, allowing it to browse freely, he quietly walked up to the edge of the stream. Using trees to hide behind, slowly walking up behind a nice sized one which was at the streams edge, he peered around it and could see three trout holding in a small hole, not more than knee deep. It had been sometime since he ate meat for a meal, especially a hot cooked meal, so he decided to see if he could catch some.

As he did not want his clothes all wet again, he stripped down, then watching from behind the same tree, he started to slide around it, towards the stream. He knew what was about to happen. As soon as his head and shoulder started to clear the tree, being exposed with nothing between him and the stream, the trout were gone. It looked like no more than a flick of their tail, and they were gone, like shooting stars across the horizon, just a blink and gone. He read in a book about hand sucking for fish, but he had not the opportunity before this time, to give it a try. Two of the three he saw go under the same rock. Slipping his left hand into the hole they went in, he put his right hand in front of another hole on the other side of the rock that they may try to escape from. Before he knew it, one of the little trout came out a side hole, hitting his leg above the knee. The second then shot out past his right hand like a bullet, going between two of his fingers as it went. He tried to squeeze on it, but it shot through with no pause. Seeing the next rock that one went under, he tried again. Visually he did not see an exit, but as he pushed his left hand in under the rock, the little trout shot out the back side of the rock, with such force and speed, that it beached itself inches out of the water on the bank. It was a little sandy area, a foot or so across, but there that trout was, waiting to be captured. Being barefoot and the rocks slippery, Maqoom did not want to break a bone, so he did not move like he normally might have, but with much more deliberation. The trout started to bounce itself off the beach, like it was swimming in air. The impact of its head hitting sand and then its tail, along with it knowing the direction it wanted to go in, aided by the slope of the bank towards the stream, it was back in the water in seconds. Maqoom reached for it, as the trout was re-orienting in water so shallow, that its dorsal fin was in the air. The only thing Maqoom got to feel, was the swoosh of the water across his fingers, from the waving of its tail. He smiled as he watched the trout swim out towards the head of the hole, up through the riffles, disappearing into the green of the next hole.

The next hole was somewhat deeper, some halfway up his thighs. Any fish that was lounging in here was long hidden, before Maqoom took his first step into this new abode of the trout. There was a nice rock with what appeared to have one opening, facing out towards the deeper water. By the time he got his hands under the rock, he was up to his armpits. As he pushed both his hands back, he had to tilt his neck to keep his face out of the water. His left fingers touched a smooth side. Then his right fingers did as well, this time feeling the fish trying to swim away. He pushed forward with both hands trying to pin it between the rock, ground and his hands. This fish was bigger than the others. Getting some control over it, he slid his hands along its body, towards its head. Taking the fingers of his right hand, he got two of them into the gills of the fish. Closing his fingers then, as best as he could, since the earth below and the rock above, was preventing him from closing tightly, he had to plow through the earth, moving dirt and small pebbles as he did, dragging the trout along closer to him, until there was enough gap under the rock to actually close his fingers completely into a fist, pulling out the trout into the air. What a beautiful fish. Blazing orange spots, deep purple hues on its back. The whitest white on its belly and edges of its fins. This one being over ten inches, Maqoom had his meal. Realizing he had a smile on his face, he looked up at the blue sky, saying "Thank You!" He then looked back at the fish.

There was guilt within him for thinking he was going to kill this beautiful creature. He kept his fingers tight, but laid it back in the water, to keep it moist. To keep the colors from fading. He did not want to kill it. He wanted to let it go. He almost had an ever so slight moment of wanting to cry, but stopping it, he continued to look at the fish in all its glory that God gave it. He pondered that a moment, '...glory that God gave it', went through his mind over and over. He read in the past about the Glory of God, but never really grasped what it meant. The fish could not see how beautifully it was created. Just like the sun, moon, stars, majestic mountain peaks, expansive seas the whirlwind and tempest, all could make a human stare with awe, but that is not their purpose. The purpose is to bring glory to God. But God does not need glory, nor can a human do anything to or against God. What is the reason? The glory is to bring man's attention to the fact that the Creator is absolutely awesomely beyond anything we can contemplate. Once the man has his attention on the Creator via all this creation glory that is inspiring him to think of his Creator, then the glory is actually bringing the human closer to a better relationship with his Creator. The glory actually draws the human close to God for the human's benefit. That is what his readings in the past were telling him, but his own limitations at the time prevented it from sinking in to understanding. Now that he was living it, the Glory of God became clear. To draw one's attention to God, recognizing all that was being perceived was created by God, all for the purpose to bring the human closer in relationship with God for the human's benefit. Maqoom's smile was so big he felt his cheeks all bunched up at each apex of the arch of his mouth. Maqoom looked back at the fish in hand. Oh, how can I kill it he thought.

He thought about the Garden and wondered if we would have killed fish before the fall. Looking at the glory God gave it, brought him closer to his Creator, but also eating it to sustain life, then give his thanks to God also brings one closer to the Creator. He had not read or been told if we would have or not ate fish before the fall, but we do now, so he was going to keep it. He did know that people did not eat warm blooded meat until after Noah, so maybe fish were included too. Going back for his knife, he moved the trout to his left hand, belly up. Slitting the underside from its back towards it head, he removed the internal organs, cutting them free. He tossed them back into the stream from whence they came, so that other stream creatures like crawfish and dragonfly nymphs as well as other fish could eat them, surviving another day. God provides for all he thought. He could not help but see the irony in his thoughts. He almost shed a tear over killing this trout to eat. Yet, he had no feelings or emotions over the 15 dead men he left lying on the road. They were created in image of God, the trout was not. Shed man's blood, by man shall your blood be shed, went through his thoughts. He honestly did not know what to do. Looking up again at the blue sky, he watched and listened. How many others have killed, believing that what they were doing was right? He kept looking up, trying not to justify anything on his own; trying not to think but remain silent, in word and thought. He knew there was right and wrong. He knew he had the ability given to him to stop some wrongs. Until he was taught differently, he planned to continue to help others by trying to stop those who would hurt them. He verbalized asking for clarity in this matter, to do what was kind, just and righteous. He did not want separation from his Creator, it was not his will. He stared up, until a calm had enveloped him, smiling ever so slightly, he faced back to the task at hand.

He looked back at the trout, letting it roll on its side in the palm of his hand, so he could gaze at the created beauty of this creature. He thought of a lesson he learned, that when saying the blessing to the Creator for this provided meal, the trout would be serving its purpose in being created. Its presented beauty would be a part of Maqoom's thoughts and the meat would help sustain a human, created in the image of the Creator. The song of this fish, doing that which it was created to do, as it did day and night its whole life, as well as what it was going to do in helping to sustain Maqoom, would join in the song of all the other of creation, culminating in bringing oneness with all and with the Creator. Maqoom intellectually understood the thought of the fish having merit in that it got to fulfill the sustaining of man, who is created in the image of the Creator. But, because of his human limitations, he was not fully conceptualizing within his conscious understanding the oneness concept, which can occur by killing and eating this fish. He knew it existed, but he also knew that the limitation of this knowledge was his own limitation. The knowledge of the existence of the Creator, one can know. But, the areas where there is intellectual, conceptualizing grayness, one has to have faith in the Creator, putting one foot in front of the other and keep going. Learning as you go, changing appropriately as you learn; always striving to get closer to the Infinite Creator, to that place of oneness with the Divine.

He wanted the fire to be out well before dark, but only had a couple hours to make it happen. Getting a fire going, with nice dry twigs and branches, he had very little smoke and a nice hot fire going in minutes. Taking a small branch, sharpening the thin end to a point he stuck it through the mouth and throat of the trout, then puncturing into the body cavity meat, towards its tail. He then laid the twig on another Y, stick which he seated firmly into the earth. Taking the opposing end of the branch with the trout on it, he laid that on the ground, taking a rock and covering it so that the trout would not fall into the fire. The trout was about a foot above the flames, angled head down. Allowing it to cook, with moisture drops sizzling in the fire on occasion, he had his meal in a short time. He flipped it two times, to try to make sure it was cooked all around. Lifting it from the heat of the flame, he tested it by pulling off the skin. It came easily. The meat went from a reddish to more brownish and was flakey. It was done. He said a blessing and ate it slowly, chewing each bite more than necessary, to increase his gratitude for such a delicacy. It laid in some wild cabbage he had found, with the cabbage laying in his hand. Before he was done, he tossed water on the fire to put it out, drenching it quickly to reduce any smoke that may be seen. He then finished his meal, as darkness fell upon his side of the earth. Finishing up the meal with some of the cabbage, he was sated. Looking up and giving thanks, a broad smile spread across his face, as he started to think of sleep. Washing out his mouth thoroughly with clean stream water and using the brush his mom had given him to brush his teeth, he was ready to retire. Smiling again, as he realized he did what his mom would want him to do, in that he cleaned his teeth. There was sincere gratitude within him for her and a hope that it was all going well for her and those around her. He verbalized, "Heavenly Father, any good that I may be used to perform in this world in helping others, please have it be accredited to my mother and my father and all their families to all generations, as meritoriousness and righteousness both in this world and in the world to come for all eternity." He stated his "Amen."

As he lay looking up at the stars, he drifted off with a smile on his face and gratitude in his being. As consciousness was leaving him, his thoughts were on the ability the Creator has given for those living to cause effect, both good and bad on those who have come before, are, or will be. Whether they are dead, living or not yet born, a living person can affect these co-souls current state positively by their thoughts, words, deeds, actions or inactions. It's always important for one to be both externally and internally self-aware of one's actions, as well as one's intent and thoughts. Even unconscious intent was important to master, as it can affect one's relationship with the Creator as well as fellow human beings and all of creation. Not only can those living cause effects in others that have been, that are or may be, but those that have been or are to be can cause effects in those alive, even generations or millenniums later. In his semi sleep state, Maqoom thought of Samuel, King David, Moses and President George Washington. Things they did, how they handled themselves are affecting him today in his drives, will, how he handles himself, what he thinks, all in positive ways. This too he quietly verbalized, as "any good I may have done or will do on account of them, please have it be attributed to them and their families to all generations, as meritoriousness and righteousness both in this world and in the world to come for all eternity. Amen."

All of creation is one, with the Creator, constant, always. There is no separation. Not across the timeline, not across distance, space nor any dimension one could think of. The Creator is One and all is within the Creator. There was a conscious recognition that his physical lips were curled back and up in a smile, as he was aware of the cheek muscles contracted to pull back that smile, feeling the stretch of the skin and lips. This being his last semiconscious thought before drifting into full sleep.

Chapter 19
Charlie

He awoke more like his usual, just minutes before the first glow of the sun would show upon the Eastern horizon. His first conscious thought was to verbalize the Creator's Oneness and give thanks for allowing him to awake to a new day. He then noticed an ever small yellowish orange break in the Eastern darkness, through the trees. He thought of the Atlantic coast, of which he was hoping to see someday, that the sun was probably full light upon it by now. He stretched, wondering if his smile was new or if he kept it all night through sleep. This thought made him half chuckle. "Good morning," he said looking up with his arms stretched towards the sky, palms open and upward. "Thank You for Your nights rest and for Your protection." Holding his arms aloft, peering at the last of the fading stars as light replaced darkness, he was calm, he was at peace. Thanking the Creator for such peace within a human, he knew he had to move on, so he did. Never wanting to leave when such peaceful states were upon him, he knew he had to though. He did not want to, but being in this realm of existence, he knows he has to, so he does.

The horse was in his usual close proximity to where he was the night before, except standing under a tree to keep the dew off him. That is one relaxed horse Maqoom thought again, shaking his head slightly from side to side, while smiling and looking at the horse who was now looking at him, with Maqoom's movement pulling the horse's attention to him. Maqoom stood, stretched and as he stepped towards the saddle stated, "It is time to go." With the horse ready and all his belongings stowed appropriately, he was in the saddle. Nudging the horse forward, he was continuing on his plan. His hunger kept him on the lookout for edibles, but his primary thought was on Charlie Brandt. As he had contemplated so many times before that he wanted Charlie wild to help cull his own men, that plan was unexpectedly crushed before it had time to materialize, with Charlie only having two men remaining. Maqoom, always on the lookout to be grateful, looked up to the ever lighting sky stating, "Thank You for helping with the success of getting most of the group and not getting hurt myself in the process."

As he rode, the smell of wildflowers filled his nostrils, with the morning dew evaporating, helping to carry their scent. The ever present birds were filling the air with their symphony of sounds. With the scent of the flowers and plant growth, came along the realization of clean air. The air was fresh, crisp, almost unconsciously pleasing to the nostrils and lungs. The warmth of the sun's rays, pushing against the coolness of the evening chill, was a very comfortable atmosphere to be in, for a human with clothes on. That thought made him think of a book of his mother's by Thomas Payne entitled Common Sense, where in the book, Mr. Payne states something along the lines that "Clothes and government prove how far man has fallen."

Neither were necessary in the garden, but both are with us now, as they are required in our current state. With that thought Maqoom looked up, "Apologize to You I do that humans have to have either of those items, because of our fall in the Garden, but, Thank You for Your kindness in giving us both for this current realm of existence." He inhaled deeply, letting it out slowly through parsed lips, this seemingly, he has experienced, to allow his physicality to calm down to the point of meeting his already calm soul. When there is harmony, calmness, joy and peace; there one is ready to meet the Divine. Maqoom knew within himself that this was an internal state of full being, not necessarily dependent on what is going on around a person, but the outside can affect such state either positively or negatively, so one must guard one's space and where one places one's self.

The small feeder stream cut into the larger stream, some ways back, as now he was crossing the larger stream again. As he cleared the far bank, his vision picked up and his mind registered, there was a large clearing ahead. Coming to the edge of the forest, there was a large field, with knee high grasses for say one hundred yards, then a wooden fence around a very large pasture with some horses and cows out feeding within. Looking at the stream-line, how it cut the forest, he could see that it went Westerly, then cut South to go behind the house. Instead of taking the stream, Maqoom was going to watch for activity from a corner post of the fence, which was well over 200 yards away from the house. His thoughts of a plan then included slipping across the field or around the fence line after dark. With the barn being between the house and the pasture, he was currently planning on slipping into the barn to catch Charlie and his men there. As the sun was getting low in the Western sky, two forms appeared from inside the house, stepping out onto the house porch. They both disappeared behind the barn, then appeared some 20 minutes later, both with a pale in their hands. Must be taking in water from the well, he thought. Both were women, with the taller of the two carrying a rifle the whole time. They both then appeared on the porch again, taking chairs and rocking the last light away. The woman with the rifle had the weapon leaning against the house next to her chair. Maqoom had to presume that she was proficient with the gun. Maybe he had four to kill now, but he was hoping it did not come to that.

Maqoom unsaddled and unbridled the horse, so it could be free if he did not make it back. Going to the stream to wash up some and fill his canteen, he headed toward the barn. He had to guess that the armed woman would look out on occasion, trying to determine the status of the evening around the house, so he went along the fence, taking the long way, first heading south, walking towards the road that led to the house. At this corner he turned with the fence, continuing to follow it west, which at this point was basically parallel to the road, getting him closer to the house. The last turn had him heading north, towards the barn, with a blacksmith building between him and the barn. It had been full dark for some minutes, with no moon showing as of yet, but in a sense of caution, this is where he stepped inside the fence, so that the fence would continue to break his form, in that now he was on the house side of the rectangular fenced area. This brought him to the back of the barn, as the back of the barn was not only a wall for the barn but used as this section of fence for the pasture, with the wood planked fence picking up again on the north east corner of the barn. There was a door on the pasture side, which was latched, so he had to slip under the fence going into the barn through the main entrance, located on the south end. He kept close to the barn with his right side, walking slowly but purposely, going around the south east barn entrance post like water around a rock, his ears open, eyes scanning from immediately in front of him to as far as he could see into the dark innards of the barn, looking up at the upper hay loft while at the same time peripherally scanning the right corner where he was intending to head. With the right, south east corner clear, he put his back to the wall, sidestepping into the corner. Tucked into the corner, in a full stand, he was still, watching, listening for any movement. It did not take long to clear the ground level of the barn of danger, with his sight, already being in nocturnal mode from the evening walk, which helped drastically in helping his eyes to adjust quickly to the added darkness within the barn. After less than a minute, he could already see clearly into the far, opposing corner that it was clear of human form. Past the pasture door on his right, there was a stall, with the back right corner being open, containing wooden saddle horses, to lay their saddles on, a tool bench along the side wall of this corner section, with an easterly facing window above the bench, that Maqoom did not notice earlier. He shook his head as he realized missing that window was a real mistake, which could have cost him his life. The conception of his trek started on the opposing side of this window, on the eastern side of the pasture, where he walked openly along the outside of the fence, believing the barn would cover his movement, as it was between him and the house. Thankfully, it appeared that no one was watching and ready.

There were two more stalls to the left of the open corner, covering the remainder of the back of the barn. Another side door facing the house, with a second floor hay loft which covered from the back wall, half way out over the ground floor. After covering the whole ground floor, he went into the hay loft, verifying there were no hiding spots up there. Coming down, he picked his spot, being the center stall in the back of the barn. The stalls were clean, with the whole barn being very tidy. He did not know if the women kept it this way or if Charlie was just a tidy man, but either way, it was very well looked after.

Maqoom had enough sustaining victuals and water for two days and an evening. If nothing occurred by the second evening, he would have to trek to the stream for more water, with the day after that being on the lookout for roots and greens.

Before daylight, Maqoom was in the hay loft. He had to use hearing only, as there were no openings to the outside from the hayloft on the house side, with the barn being well built, with the boards tight, not much shrinkage occurring over the years. There was a small crack between two though, that allowed him to use one eye, peering through the crack to be able to see at least one chair on the porch, then moving his head to see the other chair. The women had their routine, coming out in the morning, to feed the chickens, the woman with the rifle looking into the barn and surroundings. Seems like Charlie has taught her well. They would both then carry water inside. Before lunch they would both take a walk down the road, going almost to the tree line then coming back. Before dark, they would feed the chickens again, carry in more water then sit on the porch and chat before full dark. They did not talk loud enough for Maqoom to pick up what they said, but it seemed like amicable, casual conversation.

For a place to go to the bathroom, Maqoom saw a feed bucket, which he took up in the loft with him. After using it he would cover it with a canvas sack that was hanging on a stall board. Since there were no animals in the stalls, he did not want smell to tip off the woman with the gun that something was amiss.

The next morning, the women kept to their regimen. After the women went in the house, Maqoom got down from the loft, taking a stool to the edge of the main opening, away from the house, to sit and watch. From this corner, Maqoom could see the point where the road leading to the house went into the tree line. About the time that the sun was full up, the chickens had cleaned up the extra feed thrown to them and the wild birds were starting to settle down into the normal routine of the day, Maqoom caught a conscious sense that something moved. He was not looking directly at the tree line opening, so he turned that direction to see three men on horseback fully clear of the trees, heading towards the house. This time Charlie was not in the lead, but in the center of and slightly behind the other two. Maqoom put the stool back where it was, went back into the barn so his back was against the center stall, standing with his rifle ready. The blacksmith building, whose back was also a part of the fence, was open on the side facing the barn, but not open on the side facing the road. Hence the men could not ride straight to the barn opening but had to follow the road going out of sight as they went behind the building, which once they were clear of, they could head straight to the barn opening. There were also two hitching posts in front of the house, so Maqoom was not sure who would do what, but he was standing where he wanted to stand.

All three turned towards the barn opening, with the two in front pulling ahead of Charlie slightly more than when they came out of the trees. The two reigned their horses to a stop at the barn entrance, side by side just feet apart. Charlie was just coming into view behind the rider on the right of Maqoom, when Maqoom's rifle barked out its fire and lead. He took the rider in the sternum, intentionally aiming with the intent to have the exiting projectile sever the spine. The man was just picking up his right foot to come over the back of the horse to dismount when the bullet took him, in the sternum. The bullet hitting bone, pushing its way through, jerked the man back in the direction he was already intending to go. Because he was slightly twisting in preparation to dismount, the bullet existed just to the right of the man's spine, nicking it as it went by, completely shattering an attached rib, breaking it loose. Some of the shattered bone and body spray following the bullet's path, slapped Charlie on the left side of his face, with Charlie jerking his head to the right and out of the way, closing his eyes. Before the first man's tail bone hit the ground, the second man already had a bullet through his sternum, which did hit the spine, throwing the man's shoulders forwards slightly as the bullet buckled the spine as it punched through, blowing out the man's back, smacking into the wood of the blacksmith building, breaking through the board wall continuing on out over the road.

Charlie was jumping off his horse to the left side, Maqoom could tell, wanting to head to the house. Not even trying to pull his pistol. Again, he had the horse between him and Maqoom. Maqoom ran out the side, pasture door, down the half length of the barn to the open fence, pivoting through the middle and top rung of the fence boards, stopping at the corner of the barn to see Charlie sprinting towards the house. Maqoom took aim for Charlie's two moving legs, just below the hip, squeezing the trigger. The bullet took Charlie through both legs, completely busting the bone in the right one, going through meat in the left one, blowing out hitting the ground beyond. Charlie hit the ground hard, his facing smacking into the packed down earth, bouncing back up, as the energy from the fall, hitting such a solid object as the earth, made the head bounce back up slightly.

Charlie yelled out one of the woman's names, which Maqoom figured would be the taller of the two that carried the rifle. "Margret, Margret help, get out here with your rifle!" "Margret!" Charlie yelled, looking up towards the house, lifting his head and shoulders off the ground to yell it, straining so that his face turned red, as he vocalized the ending sound of her name until his lungs were empty of air, then falling silent, dropping his head and shoulders back to the ground again. Why yell for the woman, Maqoom thought when he has a gun on his side?

With no sign of the woman at the door, nor at any window, nor at the edges of the house, Maqoom stepped out into the open, towards Charlie. Maqoom was fully engaged with his surroundings, intensely aware of everything that was going on or not going on. Charlie still had not gone for his pistol, even though he noticed Maqoom walking towards him, with Charlie immediately looking away from Maqoom, back towards the earth. As Maqoom got close enough that Charlie could hear the earth crunching under Maqoom's boots, Charlie yelled, "I do not want to die! I do not want to die, you hear me!"

For as easy as it was for Charlie Brandt to murder people in horrendous ways, Charlie Brandt was afraid to die. He wanted to live. Maqoom thought, why could he have not shadowed that desire to live upon his victims? Maqoom walked up to beside Charlie's head and sat down on the ground with his feet to his right, towards the house, right leg slightly over his left foot. He used his left hand for support, placing it on the ground, slightly leaning his body to the left, with his right hand holding his pistol. From here he was close and intimate with Charlie, as well as he also could see the house from his peripheral vision, getting much clearer images with a slight twist of his head. He heard the door knob turn, with the latch sliding out of its catch. Slightly twisting his head, he saw a rifle barrel coming out first, angled down towards the ground in an approximate forty five degree angle. Next came the carrier of the rifle, followed by the second woman. They stepped out into the middle of the porch then stopped, standing silent, not moving, the gun not coming up, but she was facing Maqoom.

Charlie started to appeal to Maqoom. "I got money and you can have it all. You can have the ranch, the whole thing with the livestock, wagons and all. You can have the women too!"

Maqoom squeezed the trigger of his pistol. The end of the barrel was no more than an inch from Charlie's temple. The bullet entered in, easily churning through the brain material inside, forcefully breaking out the far side temple with an enlarging cone of brain matter spray being pulled out behind the exiting projectile, with the rays of the sun glistening off each moist droplet. Maqoom briefly moved his eyes enough to catch site of the rifle barrel, still pointing towards the earth, with all four feet not moving. He looked back to the brain material, with its glistening reflections, with even the smallest droplets now succumbing to gravity falling back to earth. Each glistening droplet lighting upon the dust of the earth, like little goblets of frost, ever so gently coming to their resting place, upon which after hitting the ground, they each one soaked up enough earth, as to dim their reflections. Maqoom watched as some of the larger droplets changed from glistening moist to dull, dry brown as the earth swallowed each like a whale feeding on the small life forms that Maqoom read they fed upon.

Again Maqoom, moved his eyes, to verify what all his other senses were already telling him, that the woman's rifle was still in its original position. Maqoom sat there for a time, looking at Charlie. There seemed no way to Maqoom, that he could have allowed him to live, especially with a clean conscience. Why did he shoot him in the legs, and not kill him outright with the first rifle shot? Maqoom was puzzling over that, when the women started to move down the porch steps, coming over to Charlie's body. Maqoom stood up, turning slightly away taking some steps towards the barn to put some distance between them and he. He kept his gun in his hand.

Chapter 20
Freedom

The woman with the gun, looked up at Maqoom, stating, "We have to get out of here!" There was desperation in her voice. "There are at least a dozen other men out there and we have to get out of here, now!"

"They are all dead." She looked at him in disbelief. "Five days ago, five of them died in town, then two days later 15 more on the road outside of town, with the last three today. The only two I know to still be alive are the livery man and the banker. It is my opinion the livery man is no threat to you. I do not know about the banker, what do you say?"

"We were not allowed to leave, so neither of us know who the banker is. The livery man though does seem ok, as I have heard Charlie talk to Ben that he did not seem to be one of them and maybe he should be killed. Ben seemed to be inclined to keep the livery man alive though. Ben did try to protect people that way, though not pushing to far which would have gotten himself dead."

"Well I have no real plans on what is next after this, so I'll tell you both, I will work to get you both where you want to go, alive and unmolested if that is your choice, before heading out on my own. Another option is you keep this ranch, making it your own."

Maqoom turned and walked away, leaving them to think on it. He rounded up the three horses, unsaddled and unbridled them, putting them in their stalls with feed and water. Sitting next to the barn on the house side was a wagon, so he dragged the two men, plus Charlie over to the back of the wagon. As he looked up at the side of the barn, he realized that he had missed an opening in the hay loft area, that had a latched door on the house side of the barn. Over the door was a wheel pulley, which would be very useful to haul up heavy objects from below. He walked around to look inside the barn again, realizing why he did not see it before, as they had hay piled up higher than the top of the door. He went into the loft, moving just enough hay to unlatch the door and push it out. Then he slipped a rope over the wheel pulley, pushing it along until the tag end was almost on the ground, allowing the remainder of the rope to fall to the ground as well, both ends hanging over the pulley.

He dragged all three men over to behind the wagon, which he had centered under the pulley. The rifle woman asked from the porch, "Do you want some help?"

Looking up, he saw them both standing on the porch looking at him so he replied, "Yes, that would be nice."

Tying a tag end around one of the men, he asked the ladies to each grab a foot. As he lifted the body with the pulley, they pulled on the feet to keep the body from catching on the wagon. After the body was high enough, he had them walk forward allowing the body to be controlled as it swung over the wagon. He then lowered the body, untied the rope, doing the same with the next two. After it was done, he looked at the women stating, "Thank you for your help."

Looking at the armed woman he stated, "You are Margaret, but what is your name?" Maqoom asked looking at the unarmed woman.

"Buttercup." Came the reply. "It is all I ever heard

anyone call me as I grew up."

Maqoom stated, "That is too personal of a name and I will not call you that, so do you have a middle name or some other name I could use?"

"No," she replied. "Though my brother always called me sis."

"Would it hurt you if I called you that?"

"No," she said.

"Then you are Sis. Do you two know what you are going to do yet?"

"We want to leave, but we are not sure where to yet and I…" stated Margaret pausing briefly in thought. "I want to go look in on my Father's old house before leaving."

"Do you want me to go with you or leave you both?"

"We ask that you go with us. Also, I want to pay you a daily wage, as I will not ever be someone's slave again, nor will I ever have a slave."

Maqoom did not want to argue with that, so he agreed to the pay without resistance.

"We got the house safe open, with there being over five thousand dollars in there. The offer is two dollars a day, plus expenses."

Maqoom smiled stating, "Agreed."

Both of the women looked at each other and smiled, really enjoying their new found freedom and independence. Maqoom stated, "One rule, that neither of you go off on your own without letting me know where you are going. If I am getting paid to keep you safe, then I want to do my job and I will not be able to do my job well, if you just go off on your own without me knowing and able to track time as to when you leave and when you should be back."

They both said, "Fine."

He also told them, "Both of you, I want you to wear standard cowboy hats, not only for sun and rain, but to help cover your feminine side somewhat. Also, as soon as possible, both of you are to purchase loose fitting, women's riding pants, with pull over tops along with loose fitting shirts to go over the pullovers. It had to be worked out though that neither the pants nor the shirt interfered with drawing a pistol. Wherever you decide to go, I do not want to be killing men the whole way because of a man's lust."

They readily agreed.

"Fine." Maqoom said. "Tomorrow, I plan on taking these bodies into town, asking the livery man to bury them for pay. Also, I may be a couple days, because I have to try to get the other 15 buried as well. You two can ride along to check out the general store in town, if you would like?"

Margaret then stated, "We do not know your name."

"Maqoom," he said.

"Maqoom, we do not want to go to that town. Whichever direction we head, the first big town we come to, we will look there."

That means you will be on your own a couple days, but you have been before. Then my pay does not start until I get back, agreed?"

"Yes, agreed."

"Do you know how to shoot Sis?"

"No."

"Are there more guns in the house?"

"Yes, rifles and pistols, with plenty of bullets for all." Margaret answered.

Maqoom took a bucket that was used for feeding the chickens, walked out fifty paces, sitting it on a fence post. Walked back, asking Margaret to shoot it. She pulled up and shot without much hesitation at all, putting the lead through the bucket. He asked her to walk sideways for some steps, then shoot again. She stepped four steps sideways, pulled up putting another hole in the bucket. She volunteered, "My dad taught me to shoot, with Charlie demanding that I keep practiced."

"It is my request that you always have that rifle with you, loaded and ready. Also, I am asking you to work with Sis, go over the guns in the house to determine what fits her best, rifle, revolver or both, spending practice time with her, every day you can, teaching her to hit that bucket, ok?"

"Yes, I will outfit her and start her training."

"Sis, any disagreement with that course of action?"

"No."

"My personal preference and a request is that both you carry a rifle and a pistol."

"We'll work on it", Margaret stated.

Sis added, "Yes," shaking her head positively.

Maqoom then pulled out a canvas tarp from within the barn, covering and cinching it down over the wagon. His plan was to pull out early the next morning, heading to town. He then went up in the loft, picking up his bathroom bucket. Climbing down, he then took hold of a shovel and another, clean bucket. Walking towards the stream and downstream of the house, he went just inside the tree line, dug a small hole, dumping his bathroom bucket into the hole. He walked to the stream with the clean bucket, filling it with water. Then he washed out the soiled bucket, making sure it was clean, pouring the dirty water into the same hole as his waste. He then covered the waste with dirt, taking both buckets, clean, back to the barn.

The ladies were nowhere in sight, of which he hoped

they were in the house, taking seriously the gun situation. He wanted Sis to be able to take care of herself, if necessary. That little lead bullet can take down a mighty big man, from just a little finger muscle action. With the help of the Creator, keeping her head about her, she could be a man's worst nightmare. Of course, everything is God Maqoom knew, whether we live or die or win or lose, but we have to do our efforts on the action, with trust the whole way through. He bridled Charlie's horse, riding bareback over to where he laid his saddle. When he first rode up, he did not see the calm horse, but as he was putting his saddle on Charlie's horse, it came walking over. He smiled, rubbing it between the eyes on its forehead, he did not know if to take it or leave it free. He thought it might be a fine horse for Sis though, so he put its halter on, leading it back to the barn. The sun was going down as he was approaching the barn, with the ladies on the porch going over the gun situation. Margaret shot from the porch hitting the bucket, almost 90 yards, with Maqoom fully realizing she can hit what she is aiming at. The ladies went in the house, Maqoom went into the barn. He had a nice spot up in the hay loft, with his intent to turn in early and get an early start to town.

Chapter 21
New Beginnings

The yellow was just starting to show in the East, when Maqoom was stepping up on the wagon seat. As he was stepping up, he noticed Margaret was walking towards him. She handed him up a small package. "Egg sandwich," she stated. "For the ride."

Maqoom let out a verbal "Wow, thank you very much; it is still warm too. Thank you again," he said with a smile, using the reins to nudge the horse forward.

As he got out a way from the house, he stated his blessing, eating the sandwich slowly, enjoying its taste and warmth, watching life all around him wake up to a new day. Washing it down with some well water, he gave his thanks, leisurely taking the rest of the ride to town as if it was an outing. At one point, he made a mental note of some wild raspberries growing just off the roadway, of which he intended to stop and pick on his way back.

As he cleared the tree line, coming into the clearing before town, he saw no humans. Making the slight turn, to come in line with the roadway through town, he still saw no human life. Bringing the wagon to a halt in front of the livery, he immediately stepped down on the ground, got up close to the wagon, standing still, listening, watching.

With no movement anywhere around him, no one stepping out to see who this stranger is, he started to think the town was actually just a shell with no occupants.

Stepping just inside the livery, he called out, "Is anyone in here?"

He stepped out towards the wagon again, looking over towards the bank. He had no intention of going in there alone, as he could get into all kinds of blame, if the banker was dead and the money gone. Immediately he realized he did not check Charlie's and the two men's saddle bags. He just thought of it now. Then he heard a "Hey!"

Maqoom spun around towards the voice, seeing no one. The voice came out of the building next to the livery. Maqoom worked his way to the other side of the wagon, putting it between the voice and himself. "Whoever just called out 'hey', this is Maqoom, please come out where I can see you."

"Is anyone else with you?" the voice said.

"No, I am alone."

There was a board creak, then the livery man cleared the doorway of the building, stepping out onto the boardwalk. "What are you doing back here?"

"Charlie is dead, along with his last two men and I came to ask you to bury them."

"You have them in the wagon?"

"Yes," with Maqoom uncinching the cover, tossing it to one side of the wagon, exposing the three bodies. The livery man came down, to verify that Charlie was actually one of them.

"I cannot believe it," he said. Maybe ten or twelve times, he kept saying it over and over, staring at Charlie's body. "I have not felt this relieved, this relaxed in a long time", the livery man said.

Turning to Maqoom, he volunteered, "Charlie came into town at first light the next day, after all the shooting out in the woods. First place he came was to get me and with a gun pointing to my head he ordered me to ride out into the trees to look over what was out there and report back to him. I counted the bodies, looked over the setup and reported back to him. I wanted to keep riding, never coming back, but I was more scared of him coming after me than I was of returning and hoping he would not shoot me anyway, or worse. After reporting to him what I saw, they went from house to house making sure you were not here somewhere, then went to the saloon, not coming out until the next morning. Hearing their boots walking down the boardwalk, they went straight to the bank, with Charlie and another walking in, with the third standing outside. One shot was fired. When they walked out, I was standing in the opening to the livery, staring at them. That was stupid. All three headed straight for me. I knew I was a dead then, so I had nothing to lose, as I was at that moment more afraid of dying than I was of Charlie. Only took two steps for me to be able to grab my rifle, that was leaning by the doorway, raised it up, snapping off a shot in their direction. Not aiming, just a shot towards them. They took notice, but I did not linger, turning around I raced out the back door, with lead flying into the building. One bullet creased my thigh, but that was all. With no woods to run into, I raced down about as far as what I figured they would not see, then ducked into a building. I was breathing so hard, I was feared they would hear me, but no sooner had I thought that, when I heard horse's hoofs, hitting the earth. Quickly I went over to the front glass, hoping this was not a trick, when I saw all three of them riding out of town towards Charlie's. Guess they figured it was not worth one of their lives in order to try to kill me. Figuring they would be back someday, I was going to leave town today, hoping they would not come after me. Then you rode in. I still cannot believe Charlie is dead."

"Will you walk over with me to the bank?" Maqoom asked.

"Yes, I will."

"Glad to see you are carrying your rifle," Maqoom said with a smile. "By the way, what is your name?"

"Last name is Gantz. Samuel Bartholomew Gantz. My mother was a Christian, and she loved Samuel in the Bible. Daddy did not mind, as he always called me son or boy anyway. Mama called me Samuel though. She loved saying that name. Think she loved Samuel more than me, but she treated me very well, I have no complaints for sure."

Maqoom said. "Yes, I like Samuel too, very much. Are you familiar with him Samuel?" They both smiled, looking at each other with the mutual recognition that there was a lot of Samuel talk occurring at the moment.

"I know what my mother would tell me of him. But I have not read it personally."

"Well, I encourage you to read it all at some point."

"Have you read it?"

"Yes, multiple times, with the intention to read it over and over again."

Maqoom paused a brief moment, with Samuel in thought, not responding, so he headed in the direction of the bank. Samuel was beside him, as they stepped onto the boardwalk in front of the bank. The bank door was not latched, so Maqoom, standing off to the side, pushed the door open with his fingers. It was dark inside, so he allowed his eyes to focus, listening with his ears for any shuffling. Stepping inside, he put his back to the wall, allowing his eyes to adjust to the lower light, with Samuel doing the same on the wall on the other side of the door. The banker was in his chair, head and arms on the desk. A hole was in his back from where the bullet came out, went through his chair, making a hole in the wood wall behind. The vault was open, with no money anywhere to be seen, except some coinage on the floor.

Maqoom asked Samuel, "Do any of the men that rode with Charlie have families?"

"Definitely two that I know of personally, with a couple more that I have heard may."

"Well, we might want to round them up later, to see how well off they are and maybe give them some financial help. It never occurred to me to check Charlie's saddle bags, so the money might be in them and if so, I want to share some with the men's families."

"These men tried to kill you," Samuel stated.

"Yes, but the women and children did not and even if one of them would freely put a bullet in me, I do not want to leave them destitute, if they are in that condition. First though, the 15 out in the woods have to be buried. Will you help me Samuel?"

"Of course I will…" with his voice trailing off along with a puzzled look on his face as he realized he did not know this person's name whom he was speaking with so freely.

Samuel looked at Maqoom, "What is your name?"

"Maqoom," was the reply.

"Of course I will help you bury them, Maqoom".

"Well Samuel, since you know this area so well, where do you suggest in order to bury them all?"

"This land around town has been cleared for many years. Let's get out into the cleared land, past where any tree roots may be from the forest, dig trenches, say about two foot deep, laying all the bodies in them length wise, head to foot."

"Ok then, let's get digging," Maqoom said.

They both got shovels and picks, taking the wagon to a location somewhat close to the 15, but away from the forest roots, out in the clearing. By the time the sun was going down hard, they had enough room for 13 bodies, in three different trenches. They would each dig in a different direction, working on one trench, until an immovable rock was hit, or until the trench was as long as they deemed appropriate, then start another trench, with the other continuing on. They laid Charlie, the two men and the banker in one of the trench's, covered them over, going into town for the night.

Before daylight next morning, they were already on horseback heading out to the trenches. Out of 15 horses, eleven came back to the livery, Maqoom had one so only three were still missing. After the bodies were all buried, Maqoom wanted to spend a day looking for the other horses. Maybe their reins had them caught somewhere and if he could free them, he did not like the thought of maybe them starving surrounded by food.

Samuel stated, "That would be unusual for a horse not to be able to break free, but I would like to ride along too, if it's ok?"

"Of course it is Samuel," with Maqoom smiling, letting Samuel know that his approval was for real.

On the third morning, all the bodies being buried and covered, Maqoom and Samuel rode out looking for the other three horses. About midday, one was spotted, it being the one that was hit in the neck with that last rider that was shot. It was still standing, but had its head hanging down, with its mouth open and saliva dropping to the ground. The bullet did not kill it, hitting no major artery or windpipe, but it must have really banged its neck bone for the horse looked like it was in too much pain to do anything but stand and die. Maqoom felt guilt for the shot, as the horse was not fighting him, but here they were now, so he was going to finish it. He got down off his horse, walked over to the animal, gently touching it, laying his right hand on its neck, under the mane. The horse moved nothing but its eyes, as the left one arched up looking at Maqoom. Maqoom moved his left hand, moving it to the forehead of the horse, using his fingertips to scratch its skin gently. He stopped his finger movements, laying his hand flat on the forehead of the horse, feeling its fur. With slight pressure on his fingertips, he pushed in ever so gently, striving to make a connection with the animal, trying to let it now that another being was with it and friendly; that it was not alone. Maqoom out loud, told it "Sorry," as he started to get tears in his eyes. He could feel the heat of the liquid upon his cheeks as the tears ran down them, tasting the salt of them as they filled the valley between his lips. Pulling his pistol, pointing it in the ear canal, angled towards the brain. With the shot the horse dropped straight to the ground. Not another movement, except for a muscle quiver here or there. They took the saddle and bridle off, then cut branches, found old limbs, covering the body, finishing the covering with old leaves.

"The other two will probably be found by someone," Samuel said on the ride back.

"Hopefully someone who can use a horse," answered Maqoom.

"There were tears in your eyes back there Maqoom. As far as I can tell, you have killed eighteen men, just in this area. Also, the other five when you first rode into town. As well as you are with those guns, I have to assume you killed more before you ever got here. Did you ever shed a tear over any of the men you killed?"

"Samuel, you have to work on determining which questions are appropriate and which ones are not. If you would have asked Charlie that question, he probably would have pulled his revolver out and shot you, do you agree?"

"Yes, he probably would have. But you are not Charlie."

"Yes, I am not Charlie, but still be careful with your questions and remarks. Though you did survive Charlie all these years."

"Thanks to Ben," Samuel stated.

"Yes, Praise God, thanks to Ben," Maqoom followed with.

"That gives me another question, how can you say 'Praise God' for Ben, when you killed Ben?"

"All the answers, I do not have at this time Samuel. The horse did not leave that morning with intent to find me and torture me to death. The men did, Ben included. Even though Ben had his good qualities, that helped more than just you survive Charlie, he still did not step over to the light, in order to end Charlie's murders. Samuel, if you really like Ben, you can still influence his outcome on the other side."

"The other side of what?" Samuel asked.

"Ben and the others have changed their garments. That is a way of stating that they have departed this realm of existence, that you and I are currently riding in, leaving their bodies and clothes here, then crossing over to the spiritual realm. Just because they are dead in this realm, does not mean they are non-existent, as they are in existence, just in another form. If you like Ben and want to help him, then on occasion when it comes upon your mind or heart, start talking to God about Ben. State how Ben helped you, was kind to you, worked to keep you from being murdered and that you want the credit for all that good work to be attributed to Ben. It is like you are testifying on his behalf before the Court of Heaven. Even if he is in torment, the Heavenly Court may ease his torment for a time or permanently, from your testimony.

"Even your mother too. At times, you can address God testifying to all the good things she did for you. Anything you can think of or testify to on her behalf, speak it out acknowledging that you are testifying on her behalf. Even if a spirit is not in torment on the other side, it can still be elevated to a higher condition based upon your testimony. As you testify on behalf of those who have gone on before you, you are also actually drawing yourself closer to God in this world. Just as you try to do good for those who are alive in this world, so too can you testify to try to do good for those who have crossed over. Since you are here physically, if you want or believe you should, you can testify for all your lineage, all the way back to and including Adam and Eve. They all did some good, because you are the proof that they all cooperated with the Creator and brought forth life upon God's earth; they all did their part, so you can bring that up too in your testimony.

"Even those unborn as of yet, you can testify on their behalf. If you are proclaiming before the court on someone's behalf, you can include not only their parents and grandparents to all generations, but also their children and grandchildren to all generations. It actually can become almost a desire, an actual part of who you are, to look for something good in everyone around you, so you can testify, on their behalf; on behalf of those who are here, who have crossed over and on behalf of those who are yet to be, before the Court of Heaven. Asking that their appropriate actions or inactions or words or even an appropriate smile as well as other goodness that flows from a human, can all be accredited to them and all their families to all generations, as meritoriousness and righteousness, both in this world and in the world to come for all eternity.

"Also, something you want to keep in mind, is to always be grateful. Thank the Creator for the testimonies that flow from you. Gratefulness is very important in your relationship with God. Gratefulness also works together with joy, so always try to be joyful and grateful in all things, as just those two qualities can take you to a new level with your Creator. Always try to nullify your importance within your own eyes, nullify yourself, which is what is required to make space so to speak, to make the place for the Infinite Creator to meet you in. That is basically the meaning of my name in Hebrew, Samuel. To nullify oneself to make the space, the place, for the Infinite Creator to meet me, a finite man. The sound of my name Maqoom and how I spell it in English, is a transliteration of the Hebrew letters. Hebrew is read from right to left, with the letters of my name being, Mem, Kuf, Vav and a Final Mem, מקום."

"Also Samuel."

"Yes Maqoom."

"You do not ever nullify yourself before any other human, only the Creator."

They rode the rest of the way back to town in silence between themselves. Samuel somewhere in thought, with his lips moving occasionally, speaking silently making Maqoom smile at the thought that Samuel was testifying on behalf of others, with Maqoom lifting his heart to Heaven in gratitude and joy.

They spent that night in town, leaving early the next morning, taking all the horses with them to put in

Charlie's pasture. As they made a right bend in the road, Maqoom spotted the raspberry patch up on the left side. He stopped, picking enough for all four of them to share, as Samuel kept the horses under control.

Once at the ranch, with the horses put away, Maqoom checked Charlie's and the two men's saddle bags, counting out $12,400 dollars, between all three. Maqoom verified with Margaret and sis, to make sure they did not want the ranch.

Both adamantly stated. "No, we will not stay here."

He informed them, "It is my intent to offer the ranch to Samuel and if he does not want it, maybe to one of the men's families. Also, I am going to take part of the saddle bag money, giving some to each family and Samuel."

Neither of them were disgruntled, disappointed nor gave argument against it; so he went forth with his plan. Samuel was out looking over Charlie's blacksmith shop, a natural farrier, Samuel was well pleased with what he saw. As Maqoom approached, Samuel turned toward him, stating, "A man could make some fine horseshoes here. This shop is well equipped and laid out well."

The smile on Samuels face, made Maqoom hope that Samuel would take the ranch. "Do you want this ranch Samuel?"

Samuel's smile faded, as he stood staring at Maqoom. Samuel looked past Maqoom, at the women as they went onto the porch, each taking a chair. "It belongs to them."

"Please follow me Samuel." Both men walked back to the porch. "Samuel, this is Margaret and Sis. Sis you saw in town, maybe you do not know of Margaret."

"No, I did not know of her," Samuel stated.

"Samuel says this ranch belongs to you two."

Margaret spoke, "We are leaving Samuel, with no intentions to come back this way. If Maqoom offered you the ranch, it is a valid offer."

Samuel's eyes started to tear up, so he turned and walked away back towards the smith shop. Maqoom gave him a few minutes, then walked over to him. "Just the thought of having such a nice house and property overwhelmed me Maqoom. It scared me too. How would I take care of it? Could I manage to keep it from those who would try to forcibly take it from me? It is more than I ever thought I would have to work out."

"Don't answer yet Samuel. Will you do something for me?"

"Yes, of course Maqoom, I will."

"Take a couple days and gather up the other men's families that you know. Ask them if they know of families the other men have. Find all that anyone knows about and bring them or have them come into town. How many days do you want before meeting in town?"

"Four, four days."

"Ok," Maqoom stated, "With day one being tomorrow. It is my intent to meet you and all you find in town on the fourth day. It is my desire to meet these families, making them an offer of cash, if they will take it. Do not know how much, I may offer each, but I do not want them going hungry or freezing because they do not have their husband, father with them. Did you ever put cash in the bank Samuel?"

"No, letting me live was my pay," he said with a smile now that Charlie was dead.

"Do you know of any banks that Charlie and his men robbed?"

"No, they got their cash from people passing through, killing all of them, selling their belongings, that which they did not keep."

"What about the people that built the town?"

"Some managed to get out, but Charlie would go after them and kill them. He rarely failed. Maybe two or three. The ones that did not try to run, Charlie eventually found an excuse to put a bullet in them or torture them to death. Then I am going to offer you some of the money too Samuel. You think about the ranch, if you want it or if you want to take off and go somewhere. It is my intent to give you a thousand dollars."

"For a full time, full day worker that amount is over three years pay at one time."

"Well, that is what I intend to do. You decide if you want the ranch and the money or just the money. The ladies and I are going to look over the horses, picking five, one for each of us, plus two for the wagon. At least one should go to each family you bring in, with the remainder going to the ranch or to you if you do not want the ranch."

Next morning, Samuel rode out to find the families. Maqoom rode along with Margaret and Sis to Margaret's dad's place. A small farm, some six miles downriver and West of Charlie's. On the ride, Margaret told them how her and Charlie were engaged at one time. "Charlie started to get somewhat rough with me, with my dad noticing. My dad wanted me to break off the engagement and I was leaning that way myself, of which I told Charlie. The next morning after I told Charlie that, Dad and I were in the house eating breakfast, when we heard hoofs coming up to the front of the house. Dad got up to go open the door, when it busted open, hitting Dad on the chest, knocking him back across the room and onto his back on the floor. Charlie stepped in the house, with two men following, one standing on each side of Charlie. The fall on the floor hurt Dad somewhat, as he wanted to get up, but could not on his own. He asked for a chair, which

I took to him, of which he used as a lean, making it to his feet, with most of his weight on one foot. He said his left hip was not cooperating and really hurt. Dad was nowhere close to a gun, as he always leaned it by the front door after entering the house. Dad was looking straight at Charlie telling him, 'I knew you were no good and I am glad now that I told Margaret to stop seeing you.' Charlie did not say a word. He pulled out his pistol shooting Dad in the chest. The blast of the gun made me shut my eyes and jump as the barrel was pointing in my direction, since I was standing beside my dad. The crack of the powder is a lot louder on that end of the barrel compared to when you are standing behind it. Dad hit the floor dead. As I was leaning down to grab my Father, each of Charlie's two men grabbed me by an arm, lifting me by my armpits, carrying me out of the house."

Maqoom and the ladies spent the next three days, riding horses, loading the wagon with supplies and ammunition and shooting, lots of shooting. Even though Margaret was trained by her dad, she was a natural with the weapons, both rifle and handgun. Sis needed more practice, but by the end of the third day, she was hitting her target with both weapons. Sis was actually the faster draw of the two. Maqoom rode out towards the end of the third day, wanting to spend that evening in town. He spent the night at the livery, thinking that is where Samuel would first go. The next morning, still no one showed up. Just before noon though, Maqoom heard wagon wheels turning. As he went out to investigate, there was Samuel in the lead of four wagons, each being driven by a woman with an uncertain number of children along, Maqoom could not tell for sure how many.

As everyone unloaded from the wagons, there were four women with seven children between them. Two had one each, another had two with the fourth having three. The oldest of the three being a boy, maybe ten Maqoom figured. Samuel reported, "This is all I know of, with these women not knowing of anymore either."

Maqoom had them all go into the livery, take a seat if they like, as he told them, "Your husbands, fathers are all dead and buried."

None of the women got hysterical, none of the children cried. Maqoom guessed that none of them were close to their men. "What are each of you planning on doing?"

The youngest woman of the women with one of the children, stood up stating, "I am going up North to my family. I was taken from my parents, less than two years ago, with my parents being murdered in front of me, but I am going back to where my grandparents live, both sets in the same town."

Then the woman with three stated, "We have a nice farm, well planted garden, some acreage and clean water, so we are going to stay put, working the farm."

The other two had no idea what they were going to do. They both shared that they have "Shacks for houses, no good land to speak of for a garden, barely finding enough food to eat from day to day."

"Do either of you have family you can go to?"

"No," they replied. "Both of our families were local and killed by Charlie and his men," the one responded.

The other shared, "We both went to grade school together, have known each other from our youngest memories, with neither of us knowing of any family outside these parts."

Samuel took Maqoom aside, "Maqoom, I'll take the ranch. These two families can settle in the bunk house, Charlie's men used. They can work the big garden and fruit tree spread that are at the ranch. They will earn their keep until they figure out if they want to move on, or if they want to continue to stay and work the ranch as hired hands."

"Ok then," Maqoom said.

He took the family of four, walking them out to the edge of town, then handing her three thousand dollars. At first the woman was hesitant, but Maqoom talked her into it. He also gave her a pistol, rifle and ammunition for both. Teach them young ones how to use those weapons, and for the right. She nodded stating, "I will." She then urged the wagon horses on, with the reins slapping their backs.

To each woman with one child, he handed them one thousand dollars, giving two thousand to the woman with two children. "Samuel, will you keep these families here in town with you, bringing them out to the ranch the day after tomorrow, early morning?"

"Yes, we have plenty of supplies here for us all." "When you come out Samuel, you will be coming to stay." Samuel nodded his head he understood. Maqoom took the other woman who was taking her child North, having her follow him in her wagon back to the ranch. Since the stagecoach stopped coming through Charlie's town well over a year ago, she would have to get the coach at the next town, where Samuel stated the coach still runs.

At the ranch, Maqoom introduced the newcomer with her child, with all appearing to get amicably along with one another. The day before leaving, anything anyone was going to take was loaded. Both Margaret and Sis were involved with dressing out the third woman, as if she were a doll baby with the woman having a whole new wardrobe by the end of the day. She only took what she could carry in her bag, as that would be all she could have on her travels.

Early next morning Samuel showed up with the others. Margaret was driving the wagon, with her horse tied to the back and Sis riding her horse.

Maqoom shook hands with Samuel, "Thank you for your help Samuel, you take care!"

Since the third woman was only riding to the first coach stop, they did not take her wagon, leaving it instead for Samuel or the other women, however they worked it out.

Maqoom asked the two women who rode in with Samuel, "Are you both sure that you do not want to catch the stagecoach for somewhere else?

Both stated, "No."

The younger, more talkative of the two stated, "This is our homeland and we are staying."

The more silent one of them nodded her head in agreement.

"It is settled then," Maqoom stated.

Maqoom mounted his horse, spun it around ninety degrees, looked at Samuel and smiled. Samuel smiled back, with them both raising a hand, palms facing each other in a wave. Maqoom spun his horse back around, nudged its sides, starting the move.

Chapter 22
Going Home

It was a pleasant ride out. Nice blue bird sky day, big white fluffy clouds floating along, with a slight breeze from the North East. There was not much talk, with the main focus of the women being the sense of freedom, with Maqoom enjoying another beautiful day of life. It was a calm, nine day ride to the stagecoach town. It would not be until the next day that the stagecoach would be coming through, so Maqoom got the ladies and child a room to share, at their request, with Maqoom getting a small room for himself, within hearing shot of the women. The next day the ladies went shopping, dressing themselves out as Maqoom requested; picking up a few items for the woman and child too.

Maqoom, along with Margaret and Sis saw the woman and child off. She was heading due North, where her two sets of grandparents lived. "I sure hope my grandparents will accept the child, or me for that matter." All gave their assurances, that they surely will.

"But regardless," Maqoom declared, "Please be prudent with the money. It is in small bills, so you do not have to show off a large amount of money, thereby gaining unwanted attention. It is not my intent to besmirch your grandparents, but do not even tell them what you have until you know the atmosphere is right, between them, you and the child. If it is too uncomfortable, you have enough to set yourself up in that area, but not in their same home." "Be wise," was the last thing he said to her as she turned to walk away.

With the stagecoach out of site, Maqoom and the two women headed out as well. They still had half a day remaining, which they wanted to utilize to make some distance between them and town. Maqoom as well as the women had already noticed some unwanted stares at Sis from at least two different men, neither of whom looked very friendly per Maqoom's perception. That first night out, Maqoom placed his bed roll outside the light of the fire, setting himself up where he could keep track of the women, but also see both main trails leading into their camp. Morning came with no trouble, of which Maqoom was very grateful. With at least two months or more of travel ahead of them, all eager to get moving; they were headed out before eating, instead, choosing to eat on the move.

Things were going very well, with the three working to stay on the trail away from big towns, only occasionally riding horseback into a town to get some supplies. After some six weeks, the woman were ready for a hot bath and some hot food. So, with a supply run required anyway, they made their way into the next big town. The town was busy, with lots of people out on the boardwalk, wagons pulling in empty and pulling out filled with supplies, cowhands and travelers all intermixed, it seemed like a safe place to take a rest and refresh. Maqoom suggested that the women each get their own room's so they could have some time to themselves, which they both agreed to. They got rooms, where the two women's rooms were side by side, with Maqoom's across the hall from theirs. Their riding horses along with the wagon horses were all at the livery pen, getting grained and watered well; it would be a nice rest for them as well. Having money sure helps with the niceties of life.

After two days, the ladies were reluctant to get up and get going on the trail again. Maqoom wanted to move out. "Definitely by tomorrow, day three," Maqoom stated.

They were pushing back, so Maqoom straight out asked, "Do you two want to stay? A house could be found or property purchased with a house being built and this could be your home."

Within minutes both answered, "No!" With Margaret adding, "But we are not in a hurry to leave the comfort, that is for sure."

The third morning, all three were in the mercantile store, looking for supplies, with the ladies acquiescing to Maqoom, that if they were not settling here, then they did have to get going. Sis was walking out of the store first, with Maqoom some three steps behind and Margaret behind him. All three had supplies in their hands. As Sis was stepping left to go down the boardwalk toward the livery, Maqoom's eyes were just clearing the doorway, presenting him an expanding visual of the boardwalk, as he came out into the open. Three men on the left, two by the post at the edge of the boardwalk, one in the middle of the boardwalk, stepping towards Sis. The man grabbed Sis under the left armpit, swinging her towards him, then pushing her back against the wall, hard enough it knocked the air out of her lungs; both her packages dropping to the boardwalk. Broad daylight, people all over the place walking, doing business and this guy grabbing Sis as if he is not concerned about anyone doing anything puzzled Maqoom.

Sis had been practicing with her pistol, of which both her and Margaret carried openly. Sis had enough sense to go for the gun, but the man intercepted it with Sis pulling the trigger and the bullet going into the boardwalk beside the man's foot. He wrenched the gun out of her hand, then back handed her across the face with the hand that had the gun in it. In the midst of such a situation, Maqoom still had the thought, that if this was the man's definition of courtship, he must be a Neanderthal, which for all Maqoom knew, even they did not act this way. Maqoom let drop the supplies packages he was carrying and before they hit the boardwalk, he had drawn his pistol, pulled it up to the man's head, pulling the trigger. The bullet going into the man's skull, at the top front of the man's left ear, coming out at the top right part of his head, slamming into the roof over the boardwalk, allowing a small amount of daylight to filter through where it made its exit. The man dropped straight down, as if he had no legs and was dropped from the sky. Maqoom was so close to the man that as the body was falling, Maqoom raised up his left leg, allowing his knee to slightly nudge the falling body, so that it would come to rest on its right side, away from Sis and Maqoom. Maqoom stood still for a moment, not moving at all, totally aware of the two men, with neither going for their weapon. This was all mixed up. Broad daylight, people all over, Maqoom half making a joke out of it with his courtship scenario thought, all mixed up with his anger that he felt as Sis had already been through all this kind of bullshit and it was not going to happen again, so he just killed the man. Maqoom knew instantly, that he did wrong.

He looked at the two men, telling them, "Go get the sheriff!"

"There is no sheriff here," came the reply.

"Margaret, please go in and get the store clerk. Sis,

pick up your pistol and watch my back." Maqoom did not move right or left but stood where he stood when he pulled the trigger. The store clerk came around, where Maqoom could see him. "Your town does not have a sheriff?"

"No sir!"

To Maqoom's right, rear came a voice, "I'll take care of this Fred, you can go back in the store."

A man walked up on the boardwalk, coming around to look Maqoom straight on. "Son, we do not have a sheriff here, we control crime and handle justice as a group. You probably noticed the past couple days that there is almost no one, man or woman that does not carry a gun. It is basically an unwritten code here in this vicinity. When we saw the two women with you carrying weapons, we presumed that you must be familiar with our way."

"Well," Maqoom started, "Since you are the spokesman, I just murdered a man, I want to confess my crime, as well as I want to know how it is going to be handled."

"Walking over here, I had six women and four men tell me that you did nothing wrong but were defending this woman to my right. You are free to go."

"But the action that I took was not justified, per the degree of crime that this man was doing up to the point that I shot him. In front of dozens upon dozens of witnesses, my degree of action was wrong."

"Son, no one standing here is going to convict you of a crime."

By this time, there were 30 to 40 people standing, listening to the conversation. "At least let me pay for repairs of the boardwalk roof and the burying of this man."

The man stated, "That is not necessary, as we have a

fund for that. I do want to thank you son, as I noticed and a couple others have brought it to my attention, that you angled your pistol up, so the bullet would not fly down the boardwalk through the other's. Just that alone tells me what kind of a person you are. That was very thoughtful, especially in a tense time like that. Thank you," the man stated.

Maqoom just looked into the man's eyes, put his pistol in its holster, stating "I am glad the Creator gave me the forethought to think of others in situations like this and it is my hope that the bullet did not drop on someone out there, hurting them."

"I would say it did not," the man stated. "As someone would have already brought it to our attention."

"Praise God," Maqoom said. Looking into the man's eyes, also stating, "You're welcome!"

A grandmotherly woman walked up to Sis, looked her in the eyes, putting her fingers on the side of her face, and through her hair. The woman stated, "You have a keeper with this man young lady."

Sis just smiled, with Maqoom knowing this was not the place for a story, so he said nothing as well. The woman walked away, the crowd started to disperse, with Maqoom asking the man, "Where can I go to donate to the fund that was mentioned?"

"You have to be a resident to donate son." With that, the man smiled and walked away.

Two other men had already walked up and commenced to handling the body, to get it off the street and buried. Maqoom was still dazed by this environment, but Sis and he picked up their packages, with Margaret never dropping hers, loaded their wagon, hitched up the team, riding out of town. Just as they were starting to move, a woman walked up, halting Maqoom then stating,

"You did this town a favor, killing that one." After which she turned and walked away.

The ride was quiet amongst them for the next two days. Margaret and Sis could tell Maqoom was not himself, so they wanted to give him space to work out whatever it is that he was grinding over. They rode long that second day, not getting camp fully set until after dark. It was an open sky, starry night. Maqoom was edgy, even more so than during the day. Pacing, not standing in one spot more than a couple seconds, Margaret handed him a plate of food. Maqoom stated, "Thank you!"

Margaret knew however, it was from his habit, not real, as he was not even in the same area as they at this moment, not mentally she thought. He hasn't smiled in two days, with Maqoom's smile being able to make almost anyone else smile, even in difficult situations. Maqoom walked to the opposite side of the fire, with the ladies on the other side, between the fire and the wagon, sitting on stools. Maqoom bent his knees, squatting down and as he was doing so, he was scooping his first spoonful of food. Just as he was picking it up to this mouth, a small whirlwind, just outside of the light of the fire picked up a bunch of dry leaves, swirling them around, slamming them into a tree as the circling wind wisped right into it. Maqoom dropped his plate, jumped up and spun around, having both guns out pointing towards the sound before his feet came back to earth. Margaret and Sis sat erect, almost holding their breath, not wanting to make a sound. Both were straining to see what was coming at them, but they saw nothing and did not want to move, not knowing what was happening.

Maqoom was extremely emotional. His heart was beating so hard that it was making his upper torso, ever so slightly jerk back and forth with the beats. Maqoom was breathing very hard, noticeable even to Margaret and Sis, as he was breathing large amounts of air, very fast through his nostrils, making it sound as if he was the beast they were all straining to see. What seemed like forever was really seconds, when Maqoom put his guns in their holsters, turning towards the women. "Terrified I am," stated Maqoom. "All I wanted to do just now was, what I have been wanting to do for two days and that is run. Run from the fear that has filled me. Just run! That man back there, I murdered him, I know that. Not only have I murdered him, but I have prevented any children that he would possibly have Fathered from being on this earth, as well as any future generations allowed. There are those who thought he should die and good riddance to him, but it was not to be by my hand, not for what he was doing in broad daylight in front of a town of witnesses. It was not justified for me to do the action I took. It was a test and I failed miserably."

Tears started do roll down Maqoom's cheeks. It says in the Bible, "…the sound of a rustling leaf will pursue them – they will fall, but without a pursuer." Because of my sin, I am filled with fear and because of my fear I want to run from everything and everyone. It also is written, "You reduce man to pulp and You say, Repent, O sons of man."

"Even in my sin, the Creator has not departed from me, is continuing to work with me, on me, to draw me back to closeness with the Creator. Nothing loves us humans like the Creator. It is I who have walked away from my Creator. My anger has turned me away from the Creator, it got control of me when I saw what that man was doing to Sis, allowing it to win. The thought I had just before shooting the man, was a vulgar thought. I actually said a word that I do not normally say in my thoughts. One vulgarity leads to another, one immoral act leads to another; in my case it led to murder. Before Cain slew Able, the Creator told Cain, '…sin rests at the door. Its desire is toward you, yet you can conquer it.' The anger conquered me instead of me conquering it. God loves us so much, that even at this time of my failure, the Creator is working to bring me back, not letting me out here alone, but calling me with fear and dread, in order to turn me back to the Creator."

The tears really started to flow now as sobbing took over, especially with the realization within Maqoom of his rebellion against the very Creator, Who even now is working to bring Maqoom back. Maqoom walked around the wagon to the far, dark side of the camp. Margaret and Sis could hear him sobbing, picking up a word here and there, but not hearing everything. Maqoom confessed to allowing anger to control him. He confessed to his vulgar thought which was rooted in the anger. He confessed to murdering a fellow human being. He cried, asking God to forgive him and allow him to come home, back into the known closeness of the Creator. He prostrated himself, hands outstretched before him, heading East. His tears running out of his eyes, mixing into the dust of the Earth. He wanted to come home and he confessed his sins, pleading with God to forgive him. Telling the Creator he is ashamed, embarrassed and humiliated because of his transgressions. Confessing, confessing, confessing opening himself to himself, searching his own mind for what he did, why he did it and confessing it to God.

Margaret and Sis were done with their plates when they both realized it was quiet. No more sobbing, no more spoken words, but no movement either. It was quiet. Maqoom got up from his laying upon the earth, walking back into the light of the fire. His plate had already been picked up as well as the food off the ground so as to not to not draw critters. "Apologize to you both for dropping my plate and thank you for picking it up, as well as the food."

Margaret asked, "You are back?"

"Yes, I am back, not the same person, but back thankfully."

"Are you hungry?" Sis asked.

"Yes, yes I am", he stated, with a smile coming across his face. With that smile they saw the Maqoom they knew, making both of them smile. She got him another plate, he stated his blessing and ate. After giving thanks, checking on the stock, Maqoom laid down and slept soundly.

It was two more weeks to Margaret's mother's house. As they rode up, Margaret was in the lead. A woman was sitting on the porch, whom Maqoom presumed to be her mother. As recognition spread across the woman's mind of who this lead rider was, the lady stood, almost running to get off the porch. Margaret was on the ground before her horse stopped, with the two women embracing, before either got to where the other was. The woman was crying, squeezed her daughter, burying her face in the curve of her daughter's neck and shoulder. The woman did not want to let her go, but after some minutes, she released one arm so they could turn around, with Margaret introducing Sis and Maqoom.

"Welcome!" the woman said, with Sis and Maqoom responding appropriately.

The woman looked at her daughter, "When you departed from here with your daddy, I did not ever think I would see you again. How is he, your Father?"

"He is dead Mama, murdered. I'll explain later, ok

Mama?"

"Ok. Are you home to stay?"

Margaret delayed her response, as a horse rode up with a woman on it and two more persons were heading their way, but farther out. The woman rider, jumped off her horse, ran to Margaret hugging both women, with tears running down her cheeks. "This is my younger sister," Margaret blurted out to Sis and Maqoom, with tears now forming in Margaret's eyes.

The other two rode up, both men, Margaret's two brothers, both with large smiles on their faces. Margaret introduced Sis and Maqoom to her siblings with hellos all around. Before anyone else could say anymore, Margaret turned to her mother, "Mother, I want to answer your question now. If you will allow me and if my brothers and sister will allow me, yes, I am home to stay. May I come home to stay?"

Mother and sister grabbed Margaret so hard, they squeezed air out of her lungs. One of the brothers stating, "Not so hard you could break a rib."

Both brothers were smiling. Margaret swung the pack of three around so she could see her brothers. "Is it ok with you two?"

"Margaret, this is your place as much as ours and yes, we want you to stay," both nodding their approval.

Margaret looked at Sis, speaking to the group, "Sis is like a daughter to me and I want her to stay as long as she likes, being as family, do any of you mind?"

Resounding No's came from all involved.

Sis got off her horse, with sister and Mother both embracing her as their own family. Margaret's smile was broad. Margaret's sister spoke up that, "Besides Mother, I am the only one not wearing a gun," mentioning it to the group.

"We are going to take care of that," Margaret responded.

The younger brother piped up, "Are you fast with that six gun?"

"Step down off your horse and take your cylinder out."

Mother piped up, "You just got here, have not even unloaded or been inside yet and you two are competing."

"Some things never change," the older brother stated with a smile.

Margaret took her cylinder out of the gun, with the brother doing the same, both handing them to their sister. They stood about six feet apart, guns in their holsters with Mother to count to one, backwards.

"Three, two," with slight hesitation, "one!"

Margaret's gun was pointing at her brother's sternum, before he fully cleared the holster. The speed and shock took him so by surprise, that he actually half stepped back with the mental thought of having a bullet punched into him so easily that it made him take a rapid inhalation of air as well, holding it for a second before releasing it, relaxing, stating, "Wow, I did not know anyone could draw that fast."

"Between Sis and I, I am the slower one," Margaret stated proudly, with a smile that helped to bring the young brothers smile back too.

The sister noticed Maqoom had turned his horse, riding away from the group, towards the trail they came in on. "Where is Maqoom going?"

Margaret and sis both spun, simultaneously yelling, "Maqoom!"

Maqoom stopped his horse, not turning around. He knew that for him it was best to move out now, not lingering. Margaret and sis both walked up, past his horse so they could see his face. "You were not going to say goodbye?" Margaret asked.

Maqoom did not want to get emotional, but no matter how he fought it, now that they faced him along with the knowledge he was leaving, he could not hold back tears from coming out of his eyes, flowing down his cheeks. He smiled, "Yes, I did not want to cry, so I was leaving without a goodbye. Blame both of you I do for this!"

"For what?" Sis asked.

"For me crying," his smile broadening. Smiles appearing on their faces, with tears as well flowing out of their eyes. "It is my hope and prayer for only the best for both of you and your families. Don't forget to look up from time to time, letting that big blue sky make you think of your Creator, helping you draw closer to the Creator. It is my hopeful intent to see you both on the other side."

"The other side of what? Sis asked.

"The other side of this life, though none of us are in a hurry to get there; since we cannot prevent going to the other side, I have intent to hopefully see you both there. It is my hope and prayer that peace be upon both of you and your homes forever." With a broad smile, not another word spoken, Maqoom nudged his horse forward. He did not look back, looking instead at the mountain and trail in front of him, then looking up at that big blue sky smiling, being filled with gratitude.

About the Author

First off, I am a Noahide. A gentile, who has acknowledged and accepted the seven Noahide laws that G-d gave to Noah, hence to all humanity. Because of the love of the Creator within me, it is my strong desire to help my fellow humans to live better lives. Lives with joy and gladness and in true peace, true Shalom. It is my belief that any human can get to that place of closeness with the Creator, whether Jewish or Gentile. That place where there is true sincerity, true desire to be one with G-d, to be like G-d in one's character, manners and treatment of fellow humans. There are some who will not like the killing that occurs in this book. However, per my current stance in existence, I deem it as a reality of the Realm of Existence we currently reside in on this Earth at this time, believing it is a tool with which to show others, that true Shalom can only come by eliminating that which is keeping you from Shalom, as long as one does so within the confines of G-d's Creation Laws and Will.